The Puffin Book of

Bedtime
Stories

Belongs to

....

The Puffin Book of
Bedtime
Stories

PUFFIN BOOKS

PUFFIN BOOKS
Published by the Penguin Group
Penguin Books India Pvt. Ltd, 7th Floor, Infinity Tower C, DLF Cyber City, Gurgaon 122 002, Haryana, India
Penguin Group (USA) Inc., 375 Hudson Street, New York, New York 10014, USA
Penguin Group (Canada), 90 Eglinton Avenue East, Suite 700, Toronto, Ontario, M4P 2Y3, Canada
Penguin Books Ltd, 80 Strand, London WC2R 0RL, England
Penguin Ireland, 25 St Stephen's Green, Dublin 2, Ireland (a division of Penguin Books Ltd)
Penguin Group (Australia), 707 Collins Street, Melbourne, Victoria 3008, Australia
Penguin Group (NZ), 67 Apollo Drive, Rosedale, Auckland 0632, New Zealand
Penguin Books (South Africa) (Pty) Ltd, Block D, Rosebank Office Park, 181 Jan Smuts Avenue, Parktown North, Johannesburg 2193, South Africa

Penguin Books Ltd, Registered Offices: 80 Strand, London WC2R 0RL, England

First published by Penguin Books India 2005
This paperback edition published 2015

ISBN 9780143333975

Typeset in Dutch by Maniworks, Mehrauli New Delhi
Printed at Replika Press Pvt. Ltd, India

A PENGUIN RANDOM HOUSE COMPANY

Contents

The Shell-Ship

VANDANA SINGH

Illustrated by Loveleen Chawla

Once there was a girl called Jaya who loved the sea and hated darkness. She had seen the sea during a trip to Kerala one summer, and had spent the afternoon picking shells out of the sand and splashing in the shallows. As for darkness, she disapproved of it. 'When I grow up and become the prime minister,' she would declare, 'I will pass a law against the night. No more night!'

In vain did her parents and brother tell her that you could not stop the night by passing a law. They tried to explain to her that night and day were caused by the rotation of the earth, but she would glower at them and stick out her lower lip and say, 'No more night!'

One afternoon, she was pretending that their little back garden was a beach. In actual fact, there was a wall around the garden and tall

buildings on every side, with people's balconies and washing lines and noises all around. But if you have an imagination as fierce and strong as Jaya's, then there's no stopping you. Tall buildings become cliffs, and the clothes flapping on lines transform into the wings of birds, and the conversations of housewives become the cries of seagulls. So with one look Jaya made the garden wall vanish and substituted for it the great expanse of sea, while the little square of grass that was the garden, with its drooping flowers, became the beach.

'I'm looking for shells now,' she told nobody in particular, digging with bare hands into the mud of the flower bed. She had already found some small stones and half a brick. She felt something cool and smooth behind a cluster of marigolds and lifted it into the sunlight.

It was a shell.

It wasn't like any of the shells she had collected or seen. It was about the size of her two hands, shaped vaguely like a conch, and coloured a pale, iridescent blue. It was as cool and smooth as iced silk.

Jaya's eyes went wide. She examined her find from all sides but there was no opening, as you might expect with a normal shell. Her first impulse was to go running into the house to show everyone what she had found. But then she thought, let me keep it a secret for a while.

She put it on the windowsill of her little room and pulled the curtain across to hide it from view.

The day gave way to evening and then to night. Bedtime for Jaya meant that the whole family spent an hour trying to get her to bed: her father and brother told stories, her mother sang her a lullaby. After all this fuss and bother she would usually fall asleep. But tonight she couldn't. She kept asking for one more story, one more song.

'Enough, now you must sleep,' her mother said firmly, turning off the light. She opened the curtains so that the cool air could come in from the window, and left Jaya to sulk.

Since she did not have anyone to talk to, Jaya complained to the darkness. 'What good are you, Night?' she whispered angrily. 'What use is the dark?'

To her surprise, a small but stern voice piped up. 'What good?' it scolded. 'What a question! How would you see the stars without dark?'

Jaya sat upright in bed, startled. She realized that the voice was coming from the shell-like object on

the windowsill. She had completely forgotten about it. It was glowing with a silvery blue light.

'Who … are you?'

'Never mind. Come up to the window and look up at the sky.'

Jaya got up and stepped carefully towards the window. Between the tall silhouettes of buildings she could see faint pinpricks in the night sky.

'The stars,' said the voice reverently. 'In the day, the glare of your sun hides them from view, but at night they emerge in their glory. Suns like your

5

own, great spheres of burning gas, red, yellow and blue. Saptarishi in Sanskrit, Aldebaran in Arabic. The names themselves are like music, like spells spoken in the languages of your world and all the other worlds ...'

'What other worlds?' Jaya asked, fascinated.

'Many of the stars you see, child, have planets that go around them in a circle, like children dancing around a campfire. The Earth that you live on is such a planet. There are some planets that are empty of life, and others, such as yours and mine, that are filled with all kinds of creatures.'

'You're from another planet? I don't believe it,' Jaya said firmly.

The shell began to glow brighter, as though in indignation. 'All right,' the voice said after a pause. 'Don't believe me. But let's pretend, shall we, just for a moment? Look up at the darkness! The sky is a great sea, and all the stars and planets are like little islands. I am a sailor, cast into the sea of night in my little shell-ship, exploring other worlds, learning their history and their languages. So I have supped sumptuously with Socrates, and argued amicably with Aryabhata and composed couplets with Kalidasa. And now, I suppose, I am jawing with Jaya.'

'If you are really someone from another planet,' Jaya said, 'then stop talking so much and show yourself!'

'Are you ready to be dazzled?' asked the creature. 'Yes? Well, then, behold!'

A round door opened in the shell, and somebody emerged. The alien creature was no bigger than Jaya's hand. From the central body, which was grass-green and covered over with purple spots (rather like a potato at a fancy-dress party), there protruded several pale, gleaming limbs. The creature moved by cartwheeling itself over and over on these little arms.

'Ooh!' breathed Jaya in wonder. The little alien was beautiful, although stranger than anything she could have imagined.

'You have three eyes!' Jaya said, counting dark, pebbly ovals on top of the potato-shaped creature.

'Actually, I smell with them,' said the creature. 'I see with my arms, you see. And I eat like this—'

The creature opened a small mouth on the top of its head. 'You don't have any boiled karela, do you?'

'Boiled karela? Of course not!'

'In all my travels through the universe I have not come across anything as delicately delicious as boiled karela. Ah, well, let me introduce myself. My name is Andarandameko!' it said, executing a complicated dance with its arms.

'Why do you have such a long name? Why are you dancing?'

'The dance is part of my name, of course!'

Jaya giggled. She tried out a few dance steps. 'I wonder what kind of dance would fit my name,' she said.

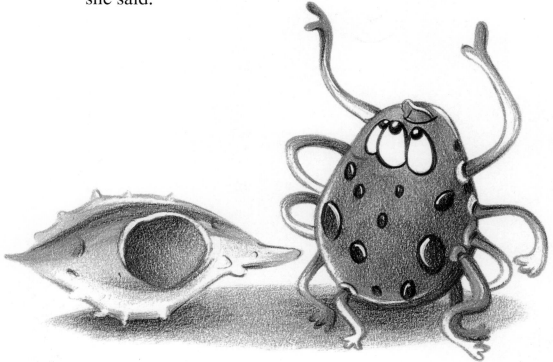

'Depends on the person you are,' said the alien solemnly. 'Come, I will tell you more about my world. Let me make a star map for you first ...'

A bubble, faintly glowing, appeared in the alien's little round mouth, and then floated up into the air. It burst with a tiny pop, and there was a little glowing star on the ceiling. Then another bubble went floating up into the darkness, and another, until Jaya felt she was afloat in space, watching the stars dance.

'I glow bubbles that blow,' said the creature proudly. 'I mean, I blow bubbles that glow. See here now, that one is my star, and around it circles my beautiful planet. Imagine its warm purple seas …'

The voice went on in the darkness, telling her of green skies, fish that wrote poetry and trees that walked. She lay back in bed and tried to imagine herself in the little shell-ship, flying towards such a world across the eternal night of space. The stars would be like great jewels, she thought, and every

planet filled with strange wonders. Half dreaming, half imagining the journey, she fell asleep at last.

When she woke, the room was bright with sunshine. She sat up in bed and rubbed her eyes.

A soft breeze was blowing through the window, making the curtains billow out like sails. But there was no shell-ship and no alien creature.

'Oh, no,' she breathed in disappointment. 'It went away. Or else I dreamt the whole thing.'

She tried to comfort herself. 'I never thought of the sky as a great sea,' she murmured. 'Or the planets and stars like islands floating in it. That means the back garden really is a beach ...' She set her imagination to work on all the games, aliens and planets she could invent and ran out into the sunshine to play.

That night, Jaya went to bed without a fuss. As she waited for sleep to come, she saw the little glow-stars on the ceiling turn on one by one. She smiled in delight.

It really happened, she thought, and dreamed of stars, planets and shell-ships all night long.

The Grand Chapatti Contest

ASHA NEHEMIAH

Illustrated by Anitha Balachandran

In the biggest, grandest palace in India, there once lived a king who hardly ever got angry. He did not get angry when the queen polished his golden crown with black polish or when she used his silver hairbrush to brush the royal dog. He did not get angry when the royal servants forgot to fill his satin pillow with fresh rose petals every night, or to line his stiff silver shoes with the softest feathers every morning.

There was only one thing that made the king angry. And that was when he was not served perfectly round, soft, fluffy-puffy chapattis for his meals. The king loved eating chapattis so much that he wanted chapattis for breakfast, lunch and dinner every day.

That was why the queen was most worried when the royal kitchen's Chief Chapatti Cook left his job and went away to the Himalayas to become a holy man.

'Who will make chapattis just the way the king

likes them? Perfectly round, soft and fluffy-puffy chapattis?' the queen asked the remaining ninety-nine cooks in the royal kitchen.

'Not me,' said the Chief Chicken Cook. 'I can make chicken curries and chicken kurmas. I can make stuffed chicken and roasted chicken. But to make chapattis just the way the king likes them—perfectly round, soft, fluffy-puffy. Forgive me, Your Highness, that's something I just cannot do.'

'Not me,' said the Royal Sweet-Maker. 'I can make sweets from milk and honey, and sweets from dates and almonds. I can even make sweets from cactus flowers and pine needles, and sweets from rose thorns and blackberry prickles. But to make chapattis just the way the king likes them—perfectly round, soft, fluffy-puffy. Forgive me, Your Highness, that's something I just cannot do.'

The remaining ninety-seven cooks had the same answer for the queen. So the poor, worried queen decided to hold a Grand Chapatti Contest. She would invite everyone in the kingdom to take part in the contest. Whoever made the best chapattis would be given a bag of gold coins as the prize and offered a job as the Chief Chapatti Cook in the royal kitchen.

That morning, the king came smiling down for

breakfast. He kept smiling till he took one bite of the chapatti on his plate and then his face crumpled up in disgust.

'Yuck!' said the king. 'This is the worst chapatti that I have ever eaten. It's stiff as my royal shield and as hard as the golden plate I'm eating on. I will certainly punish the cook who made this terrible chapatti!' He picked up the chapatti and flung it out of the window.

'Don't be angry, dear,' said the queen, hoping no one would tell the king that she was the one who had made his breakfast chapatti that morning. 'I will be getting a new Chief Chapatti Cook today! I am holding a Grand Chapatti Contest. The person who makes the best chapatti will be given a bag of gold coins as the prize and also the job of Chief Chapatti Cook in the royal kitchen. I have sent out the royal messengers with their drums and trumpets to tell all the people in our kingdom about the Grand Chapatti Contest.'

Out in the towns and villages of the kingdom, the royal messengers in their robes of pink and green and purple were telling the people about the Grand Chapatti Contest. 'Grand Chapatti Contest at the palace today! Grand Chapatti Contest at the palace today!' they shouted, banging their drums and blowing their trumpets as they walked through the streets. 'Whoever makes the best chapatti will win a bag of gold coins and be given a job as the Chief Chapatti Cook in the royal kitchen.'

In one of the villages of this kingdom, there lived a little girl called Meena. When Meena heard about the Grand Chapatti Contest, she wanted her mother to take part. Meena's father was a peanut-seller and he sold peanuts that he roasted on a little clay stove on his little pushcart. Meena's family was very poor and the only thing they could afford to eat was plain

chapattis with boiled peanuts or plain chapattis with peanut chutney, or sometimes just plain chapattis with a slice of raw onion. Since they didn't eat much else, Meena's mother always took great care to make her chapattis round, soft and fluffy-puffy. Meena thought her mother made the best chapattis in the kingdom and was sure to win the prize.

Since the contest was to begin soon, Meena's father gave Meena and her mother a ride to the palace on his little pushcart.

At the palace grounds, there were already hundreds of cooks busy at work making the most amazing

chapattis Meena and her parents had ever seen. Butterfly-shaped chapattis and spinach-flavoured chapattis. Chapattis stuffed with raisins, chapattis layered with butter. Chapattis that smelt of cardamom and chapattis that were coloured with saffron. Chapattis as soft and fine as muslin that you could actually see through, and one chapatti that was so large that it required four people to carry it.

How could her mother possibly make a chapatti that was better than all these wonderful chapattis, Meena wondered, feeling very worried indeed.

The other cooks had very special cooking vessels too. One cook had a glass rolling pin, one had a moonstone rolling board. One cook had brought along two wrestlers to help knead the chapatti dough, while another had come with his pet elephant wearing silk socks so that it could stamp the balls of dough into chapattis.

Soon it was time for the king and queen to choose the best chapatti. They sat at a special table under a striped silk tent at one end of the garden and every person who had made a chapatti was to give it to the king to taste.

The king refused to taste the butterfly-shaped chapatti when it was brought to him saying, 'I like only round chapattis!'

'This colour is awful!' he said about the green, spinach-flavoured chapatti which was taken to him next.

'Smells of elephant's toes!' he said when he sniffed at another chapatti.

Next came the fluffiest-puffiest chapatti Meena had ever seen. The cook had used a special pump to fill extra air into the chapatti after it was made. The king's eyes brightened. Meena was sure the cook who had made this chapatti would win the prize until … the fluffiest-puffiest chapatti rose up from the plate and floated off—up, up and away into the air!

The cook who had made a chapatti so soft and fine that one could actually look through it, carried it carefully to the king. As she neared the table, a petal from one of the flowers in the garden fell on the soft, fine chapatti and it tore into half.

'I can't eat torn chapattis,' said the king.

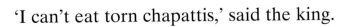

Then the king was given the chapatti filled with nuts.

'Cold and hard!' the king complained when he tasted it.

'Too hard,' he grumbled as he pushed away another chapatti after just one bite.

Indeed, most of the delicious chapattis made by the cooks had turned cold and hard before the king could taste them.

This gave Meena an idea. She asked her father to push his cart as close to the silk tent as possible. She asked her mother to sit on the cart and make the chapattis on the little clay stove kept on it.

And just as the chapatti Meena's mother made was ready, Meena's father pushed the cart right next to the king's table and the perfectly round, hot, soft, fluffy-puffy chapatti was slipped straight off the stove and on to the king's golden plate.

'Mmm,' said the king, when he took his first bite of the chapatti. He couldn't say much more as he was already eating yet another perfectly round, hot, soft, fluffy-puffy chapatti that Meena's mother had made. Then another. And another. Till he had eaten fifteen chapattis in all.

'These are the best chapattis I have ever eaten!' said the king. 'Rounder, hotter, softer and more fluffy-puffy than any chapatti I have ever tasted!'

So the king and queen declared Meena's mother the winner of the Grand Chapatti Contest and gave her the prize of a bag of gold coins. Meena's mother was also made the Chief Chapatti Cook in the royal kitchen. With the money she earned, they would be able to eat more than just chapattis and peanuts every day.

As for Meena's father, he had to buy himself a new cart on which to roast and sell peanuts. That was because his old cart was painted red and gold and put right next to the royal dining table so that Meena's mother could make hot, soft, round, fluffy-puffy chapattis for the king every day, using the little clay stove on the cart.

A Tiger in the House

RUSKIN BOND

Illustrated by Taposhi Ghoshal

Grandfather had gone on a hunting party. He did not like to hunt, but he loved wandering in the forest. He was strolling down the forest path at some distance from the rest of the party, when he discovered a little tiger, about eighteen inches long, hiding among the intricate roots of a banyan tree. Grandfather picked him up, and brought him home after the hunt.

The tiger cub was named Timothy. At first, he was brought up entirely on milk given to him in a feeding bottle by our cook, Mahmoud. But the milk proved too rich for him, and he was put on a diet of raw mutton and cod liver oil, to be followed later by a more tempting diet of pigeons and rabbits.

Timothy was provided with two companions— Toto the monkey, who was bold enough to pull the young tiger by the tail, and then climb up the curtains if Timothy lost his temper; and a small mongrel puppy,

found on the road by Grandfather.

At first, Timothy seemed to
be quite afraid of the puppy.
He darted back with a
spring if it came
too near. He would
make absurd dashes
at it with his large
forepaws, and then
retreat to a ridiculously
safe distance. Finally, he
allowed the puppy to crawl
on to his back and rest there!

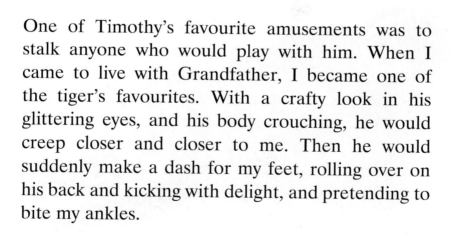

One of Timothy's favourite amusements was to
stalk anyone who would play with him. When I
came to live with Grandfather, I became one of
the tiger's favourites. With a crafty look in his
glittering eyes, and his body crouching, he would
creep closer and closer to me. Then he would
suddenly make a dash for my feet, rolling over on
his back and kicking with delight, and pretending to
bite my ankles.

He was, by this time, the size of a full-grown
retriever. When I took him out for walks, people
on the road would keep away from us. When he
pulled hard on his chain, I had difficulty in keeping
up with him.

His favourite place in the house was the drawing room. He would make himself comfortable on the sofa. He would lie there with great dignity and snarl at anybody who tried to get him off.

Timothy had clean habits. He would scrub his face with his paws exactly like a cat. He slept at night in the cook's quarters, and was always delighted at being let out by him in the morning.

'One of these days,' declared Grandmother in her prophetic manner, 'we are going to find Timothy

sitting on Mahmoud's bed, and no sign of the cook except his clothes and shoes!'

Of course, it never came to that, but when Timothy was about six months old, a change came over him. He grew steadily less friendly. When out for a walk with me, he would try to steal away to stalk a cat or someone's pet Pekinese. Sometimes at night we would hear frenzied cackling from the poultry house, and in the morning there would be feathers lying all over the veranda. Timothy had to be chained up more often. And finally, when he began to stalk Mahmoud about the house with what looked like hungry determination, Grandfather decided it was time to transfer him to a zoo.

The nearest zoo was at Lucknow, two hundred miles away. Reserving a first-class compartment for himself and Timothy—no one would share a compartment with them—Grandfather took him to the Lucknow Zoo. The zoo authorities were only too glad to receive a well-fed and fairly civilized tiger as a gift.

Sereng Yeti

ADITHI RAO

Illustrated by Ajanta Guhathakurta

'Sereng Yeti! Come to tea,
Or you will go to bed hung-a-ree!'

Mother Yeti's cry rang out from the kitchen. But little Sereng Yeti was too busy to hear her.

Where was Sereng Yeti?

Far away by the icy river, Sereng Yeti was throwing snowballs with Cecily Seal!

'Ouch!' cried Sereng, when Cecily's snowball hit him on the nose.

Cecily laughed. 'I win, don't I? My snowballs hit you five times and yours only hit me once!'

'Yes, you win. Now let's get home or Mother will be angry.'

Off they went, ploughing and wading through piles of snow.

Sereng stopped when his foot touched something soft. He felt around in the snow to see what it was.

'Hurry, Sereng! Don't stop to make snowballs now or we'll be late,' called Cecily, who had gone ahead.

But Sereng was looking down at something in his hand and didn't reply. Cecily came waddling back impatiently.

When Cecily caught sight of what Sereng was holding, she forgot to scold. It was a tiny grey creature curled into a tight ball, and it wasn't moving!

'I think he's dead,' whispered Sereng sadly.

'Let's take him to your mother. She'll know what to do,' said Cecily.

When they showed the little creature to Mother Yeti, she exclaimed, 'It's a squirrel! I wonder how he got here. Squirrels usually live down in the valley because the mountains are too cold for them.'

'Is he dead?' asked Sereng anxiously.

'No,' replied Mother. 'He's hibernating.'

'He's what-er-nating?' cried Sereng and Cecily together.

'Hi-ber-na-ting. Some animals go to sleep when it gets too cold. That's called hibernating.'

'How odd!' said Cecily.

'Shh. Not so loud. You'll wake him up,' warned Sereng.

But Mother looked sad. 'I'm afraid he won't wake now. And if you don't find a way to warm him soon, he might even die.'

Mother went back to cooking mint-leaf stew for dinner. Sereng and Cecily were left to wonder what to do. Their houses were not warm, as yetis and seals like living in the cold.

After a while, Sereng had an idea. 'Let's go to Uncle Yak-yak and ask him to warm the squirrel. He's so hairy, the squirrel can cuddle up next to him.'

Yak-yak was a good friend but he loved to talk. 'Ooh, a baby squirrel,' he said in his deep voice. 'Now that's odd. What's a squirrel doing up here? I knew a squirrel once who …'

'Uncle Yak-yak,' said Sereng quickly, before the old yak could begin one of his very long stories, 'would you warm the squirrel for us please? We're afraid he might die in the cold.'

'Of course. Put him near my tummy and he'll grow warm in a jiffy.'

31

The squirrel was tucked away close to Yak-yak's warm, furry belly, and Sereng and Cecily sat down to wait for him to get warm.

Yak-yak said, 'He can't remain here forever, you know. It is too cold for him. You will have to get him down to the valley quickly.'

Sereng and Cecily looked worried. 'But, Uncle, Cecily can't walk that far and I don't know my way down the mountain,' said Sereng slowly.

'Hmm,' said the kindly old yak, 'then I'd better take the little fellow myself.'

'Oh, thank you!' cried Sereng and Cecily, but before they could say any more, Yak-yak held up his hoof.

'Shh! I feel something stirring. I think the squirrel is waking up.'

The three of them bent over the squirrel, who opened first one eye and then the other, stretched himself and yawned. When he saw three pairs of excited eyes looking at him, he gave a little squeak and jumped up in fright.

'Don't be afraid, little one, we won't harm you. This is Sereng, that's Cecily, and I'm Yak-yak. Sereng here found you and rescued you.'

The squirrel gave them a shy smile. 'I'm Veenu,' he said. 'I guess you are my friends because you saved my life!' With a big smile he shook hands all around.

'How did you get here?' asked Sereng.

'A hawk flew away with me. It was horrible! He meant to eat me, but dropped me into this land of snow when a loud noise startled him. It was so lonely and cold, and I began to feel very sleepy. I guess I must have dozed off a little.'

'Oh, no,' said Cecily importantly. 'You were hinerbating.'

'Hibernating,' Sereng corrected gently. 'It looks like the hawk hurt you. Are you in pain?'

'A little.'

'Sereng can heal it. Yetis have magical powers, you know!' said Cecily proudly.

'I'm afraid I'm not very good at healing because I've only watched Mother doing it a few times. Let me see if I can remember the mantra.'

Sereng thought hard for a while. Then, pointing his fingers straight at Veenu, he cried:

'Ashaan fahaala minole KHARGOSH!'

Lo and behold, the squirrel turned into a rabbit!

'What happened?' cried Cecily.

'I think khargosh means rabbit in Hindustani,' said Yak-yak.

Sereng simply stood there, looking at his handiwork in dismay.

'Come on Sereng, try again,' said Cecily.

Sereng thought hard again. Finally, he said, 'I think I've got it now! Ashaan fahaala minole COHOSH!!'

This time, Veenu was a squirrel again and completely healed! He was so thrilled that he bounced up and hugged Sereng. 'You are a hero! You healed me!' he cried.

Sereng grinned. Veenu was so cute, you just couldn't help loving him!

Cecily was a bit jealous that her best friend now had such an admirer. 'Well,' she said huffily, 'you'd better be on your way.'

'Yes,' said Yak-yak, 'I'm going to take you back to the valley and we must leave at once.'

Sereng and Cecily waved to Veenu, who sat on Yak-yak's back with a lock of the yak's thick hair wrapped snugly around him. They waved until the travellers were out of sight and then turned to go back home.

'He's the sweetest little creature I've ever met,' said Sereng. But when he saw Cecily's face fall, he added quickly, 'Except for a certain little seal who happens to be my best friend.' And Cecily's face brightened again!

The next morning, Sereng refused to get out of bed and go to school.

'Why not?' demanded Mother.

'Because it's cold outside and I'm hibernating!' replied Sereng.

The Last Day of the Holidays

CHATURA RAO

Illustrated by Bindia Thapar

Creak, went Thangi's swing. *Cree-ak*, it said as she climbed on.

It was very early in the morning. The clouds were pale and the chilly breeze made Thangi shiver. The breeze woke the plants in the little woody garden. The yellow roses yawned. Dew quivered and slipped down the blades of grass and leaves.

Thangi's swing went back and forth, back and forth. She kicked the ground to go higher.

There he was, her friend the sun, peeping over the garden fence. 'Good morning!' Thangi shouted. The sun beamed back happily.

It was the last day of the winter vacation. Christmas

and New Year were over, and school would begin tomorrow. 'I want today to be as long as possible. Don't set quickly so that I can play and play and play,' Thangi told the sun.

After breakfast, Thangi played cricket with Situ–Gitu, the twins who lived next door. Gitu was batting when a buffalo lumbered up behind her. She didn't know he was there till he drooled on her shoulder! Gitu ran home screaming. Situ fell into the gutter, she was laughing so hard!

In the afternoon, Amma told Thangi to take a nap.

'Amma, please, not today! It's the last day of the holidays!' Thangi cried.

So her mother let her run about in the park with Blackie, the stray dog. They chased a cat and found some baby mice in Shambo Uncle's garage.

Blackie told the blazing sun all about them: 'Wooo, woof-wuff!' The sun waved a cloudy hand.

In the evening, Thangi skipped along the muddy track to the market with Amma. While Amma bought vegetables, the shopkeeper gave Thangi a sweet and a bun. *Slurp!* went the sun.

After a while, Thangi felt hungry. 'Is it dinner time yet, Amma?' she asked. She knew it must be too early, the sun was still too bright.

'Come to the table. It is almost seven-thirty,' her mother replied, staring out of the window as she spoke. It was very odd. The sun was shining as if it was still five o'clock!

Amma lit the evening lamps and sang a bhajan,

41

but she kept breaking off to go and look outside. It was strange to be doing this while it was still bright outside. She turned on the lights out of habit, but then turned them off again.

Appa came home from the office. 'Shanta,' he called, 'it is very strange. The sun hasn't set today!'

Thangi stood at the door and looked outside. The garden was lovely in the evening light. But the flowers and leaves were drooping. It was time for them to go to sleep. But the sun was still shining on, so how could they sleep?

Thangi rubbed her eyes. She was very tired but too excited to sleep. The sun was just like her. His edges were ringed with tiredness, but he was fighting sleep.

'You don't want the holidays to end, do you?' she whispered up at him. 'It's been too much fun!'

After dinner, Amma and Appa sat in the sunlit garden. Thangi creaked slowly back and forth on the swing. The mosquitoes swarmed around, confused. They were hungry, but it was too bright to bite!

'Why won't it grow dark?' Situ's mother asked over the garden fence.

'The sun is going to burst and scorch us black!' Situ whispered to a frightened Gitu.

Thangi's head felt heavy. She rested it in Amma's lap.

Appa turned on the radio for the nine o'clock news. The announcer said that the government weather bureau had sent their officers to a nearby hilltop to observe why the sun was being so strange.

'I can tell them why he won't set,' Thangi said sleepily, as she went indoors. She lay on her little bed, facing the open window. 'It must be eleven o'clock. I have never been up so late.' The sun looked tired and cranky too.

Then she saw something that made her sit up. The moon was floating close to the sun. At first, she was barely visible. Then she got brighter and more angry.

The sun and the moon began to quarrel. The stars crowded in behind the moon, all arguing at once. 'It is our turn to play in the sky! If you hog the playground, where will we go?'

Through watery eyes, Thangi saw a tiny star—the tiniest one—step forward. The little star asked the

sun to let her play in her cool dark pen, like she had every night for thousands of years.

The sun was a pig-headed fellow, but he had a heart of gold. He melted a bit at the little one's pleading. Then he looked sadly through Thangi's window, as if to say, I tried.

A huge rustle swept the trees. A great soft whistle rippled through bush and grass. Then the big disk sank quickly out of sight.

Sudden darkness filled the world. The sky was filled with shimmering stars. The lights came on in the houses in Thangi's lane.

Appa and Amma came up to say goodnight, but like the sun, Thangi had fallen fast asleep. That's how the winter holidays ended.

Look, a Nest!

ANITA VACHHARAJANI

Illustrated by Taposhi Ghoshal

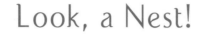

One morning, as Siya opened her eyes—
'Come here!' said Papa. 'Here's a surprise!'

Siya walked sleepily over to where
Papa was standing next to a chair.

'Hurry!' he said. 'Climb quick, my Si!
And look out at that mango tree!'

Siya climbed up and Siya looked out.
Why do you think Si gave a great shout?

Right in the middle of the mango tree
Was a bunch of twigs, stuck tight as could be!

A pair of crows flew up from the ground,
One sat on the twigs, one flapped around.

'Is it a nest?' asked Siya happily,
'Yes!' said Papa. 'For the Crow family!'

The crows were busy collecting stuff—
Twigs and leaves and bits of fluff.

Pretty plastic, some shiny foil—
They built the nest with art and toil.

Siya and Papa on the window sill,
Put out goodies their hearts to thrill!

Snap! Papa Crow would make a dash,
And *gulp!* went Mama Crow in a flash.

'When, oh when?' every day Siya
    sighed.
'When will there be eggs inside?'

One day, Papa said, 'Siya come
    here—fast!
Look! Four eggs in the nest at
    last!'

'Quietly,' he whispered, 'we
    must take care,
Or the birds will fly off
    from there!'

Siya stood there as quiet as a mouse,
Watching Mr Crow fly around his house.

Mrs Crow sat with the creamy-green eggs
Tucked safely under her chest and legs.

Now every bedtime Siya sighed,
'Tomorrow, will the babies be outside?'

Papa said, 'Patience!' every night,
'Babies come when the time is right!'

'Oh, birdies, come on!' Siya would say,
Before she nodded off every day.

One morning, Siya was pulled out of bed.
'Open your eyes, you sleepyhead!'

When Siya blinked and opened her eyes,
The nest in the tree held a lovely surprise

Four huge pink mouths wide ajar
In little grey bundles of downy fur.

And then there was so much to do!
Up and down their father flew!

'The babies want to grow big and strong,
So Papa Crow hunts all day long!'

Mama Crow stayed back in the nest,
She fed and guarded without rest.

The pink mouths were always open wide,
Worm after worm disappeared inside!

Siya watched as the little birds grew
Big and shapely, and feathered too!

Mama Crow taught her babies to fly,
Up and down the tree—not too high.

'Soon,' said Papa, 'they'll fly away,
And have nests of their own one day!'

And soon they did fly up high,
Over the trees and into the sky!

Siya watched as the birds flew far away,
Would they come back some day?

It's Hot!

MICHAEL HEYMAN

Illustrated by Anitha Balachandran

It was May, and New Delhi was hot. When Meena looked out of her window, she saw the sun hanging in a hazy blue sky. Everything outside looked tired. The plants in the garden had wilted to a brownish green. Her favourite white flowers on the hedge could barely keep their heads up. Nothing moved.

Meena put her cheek against the warm glass and looked up to the top of the tallest tree. Even the three lonely leaves on the treetop didn't stir and patiently baked under the sun. The bright-orange flowers of the gulmohar tree glowed.

Something stirred. A brown, spotty dog slunk by, kicking up little clouds of dust. It disappeared down the road.

Meena looked down at Khampa, her German shepherd. 'I'm glad we're inside,' she said to him. He lay at her feet and wagged his tail once to answer. She looked up and smiled at the fan whirring above her. It made strands of her black hair tickle her forehead.

Just as she looked back at her book, she heard a small click. It was even quieter than before. The fan was slowing down, stopping. A last gasp of air brushed her face, and then all was still.

From the next room, Meena's mother said, 'Ooh! The electricity's out again!'

'Ma, when will it be back on?' Meena shouted.

'I don't know,' said her mother as she peeked her head into Meena's room. 'It could be a few minutes, or it could be hours. We'll just have to wait.'

'Wait?!' Meena said. 'But what will I do in the meantime?'

'What do the cows do? You'll just have to bear with it,' her mother said as she went back to the other room.

Meena felt the first beads of sweat popping out on her forehead. She tried to read, but she got hotter and hotter. Finally, she gave up. 'I must do something,' she decided. 'I think I will go outside. It may be cooler. Come on, Khampa!'

Khampa jumped up, knowing that he would soon be sniffing his favourite spots in the park.

Meena called out to her mother, 'We're going to take a walk in the park.'

'OK, but don't go too far, and try to keep cool!' her mother replied.

Near Meena's house was a huge wooded park called Deer Park. Sometimes she played badminton with her friends there. It was full of tall white-trunked ash trees and secret paths that led into dark corners of the forest. One path led to a sudden clearing, in which stood an ancient crumbling tomb, with a dome on top. What Meena liked best about the park were the animals. There were white-spotted deer, cows, rabbits and peacocks.

In the park, even under the shade of the tall trees, it was very hot. Meena and Khampa sat down in front of the deer pen. Khampa panted heavily, his big pink tongue hanging out of his mouth. As Meena patted him, his fur felt hot.

Meena was worried that his panting would make him hotter. After a few minutes, though, Khampa seemed more comfortable. The deer in front of her also seemed quite cool. A black bird with a bright-yellow beak hopped by cheerfully with its mouth wide open. But Meena was still sweating and hot.

Meena remembered what Ma had said about doing what cows do. Maybe she could learn how to deal with the heat from the animals around her. Khampa's wet, floppy tongue wagging in the breeze actually cooled him down. The bird also kept its mouth open, like Khampa, but without the tongue. The deer kept cool by lying in the shade of a tree.

'Okay, Khampa, I'll try it your way first!' Meena said to him. She stuck out her tongue as far as she could and panted heavily. 'Huh, huh, huh, huh! Huh, huh, huh, huh!'

A woman in a green salwar kameez and her son,

wearing a baseball cap, walked by and stared at Meena.

Meena actually was feeling cooler! She had learned the dog's secret and now she would never have to feel hot! 'Huh, huh, huh, huh!'

After a minute or two, she had to stop because the trees seemed to spin around her, and her stomach gurgled. Worse, she started to feel hot again.

'That didn't help at all,' she said to Khampa. 'I think I'll follow the example of the bird.'

Meena opened her mouth as wide as she could, so wide that she could barely see. Just at that moment, something fuzzy landed in her mouth.

'Blaaach!'

She ran around the path, waving her hands in the air and spitting, *'Ptew, pteew, pteeew.'* Khampa thought it was a game and chased her around, barking playfully.

The mother in the salwar kameez shook her head at Meena and said to the boy, 'It's not nice to spit.'

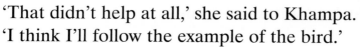

55

Meena looked over and sent an extra-loud '*Ptew!*' in their direction. Finally, she spat out what was in her mouth—it was a small, soggy leaf.

'This is no good!' she said. 'Next time a big hairy bug might land in my mouth. Yuck! Maybe the birds catch their supper this way, but I'd rather have Ma's cooking!'

Meena was no cooler, and much more tired now, so she decided to try the deer's method. She marched to the nearest tree, a giant white ash, and settled into a pocket in the gnarled roots, resting her head on a patch of soft green ferns.

It was a little cooler here, and Meena thought maybe this was the right way. She shut her eyes.

Just as she was about to fall asleep, she felt something crawling on her leg. Then she felt something crawling on her arm. Next she felt something crawling on her neck. She opened one eye. Several big black ants were crawling over her.

She jumped up, brushing them off. 'Sorry, deer,' she said. 'I can't cool down under a tree as you do because the ants will crawl all over me. If enough ants came, they might even try to carry me away!'

Meena got down on her hands and knees to look at

the ants. Surely they had to deal with the heat too …
'How do you do it?' she asked the ants.

When she had first brushed them off, the ants had run around angrily in circles, but now they were getting back to business, scouring the ground for food. She noticed that, for some reason, they raised their bottoms up in the air, and she guessed that they did this to keep as much of themselves off the hot ground as possible, and to let the breeze in under them.

'That might work,' she said and immediately got on all fours. She proceeded to crawl up and down the path with her bottom sticking up high in the air. Troop, troop, troop, troop!

Troop, troop, troop, troop!

She tried to think ant-like thoughts as she marched. She imagined the joy of finding a giant blob of grape jam on the pavement. 'Mmm,' she hummed to her ant-self.

The mother and son, who had been watching the deer, now pointed at her and laughed quietly, but Meena didn't care because she knew the ants' secret method.

'I'm an ant!' she said proudly to them.

After four trips up and down the path, behind wagging in the air, Meena stopped. 'I don't think this is working, Khampa. Maybe I need six legs like an ant. It's a bit tiring to do it on my hands and knees!'

Khampa looked back at her, panting in sympathy.

As Meena sat on the ground, wondering what other animal she could learn from, she noticed the slightest glint of light from under a rock.

'Shh, Khampa,' she whispered. 'I think there's somebody under there.'

She crept up to the rock. The glint was a lizard's eye. The lizard was about as long as Meena's hand and sat completely still, its lean brown body sheltered under the rock. Meena inched forward to get a better view. It didn't seem to mind the heat at all under its rock.

'Maybe the lizard has the best method,' she whispered back to Khampa, who was more interested in chewing a stick.

Nearby were some large rocks. One tall rock had a space underneath that looked just about big enough for her. Meena got down on her belly and crawled like a lizard under it. It felt cool

58

against her back. She pressed herself flat and tried to think lizard-like thoughts of juicy flies and handsome he-lizards. Khampa jogged over and sniffed at her.

'It's okay, Khampa. I'm a lizard!'

It was a little cooler under the rock, but after a few minutes, Meena's legs started to get pins and needles from being pushed against the hard rock. No matter how much she thought of herself as a lizard crawling through fields and jumping on tasty crickets, she couldn't ignore how uncomfortable it was being crammed under the rock.

'Phoo!' she said and scuttled out from under the rock. 'What a mess I am! I guess I don't make a good lizard.'

As Meena stood up and brushed the dirt off her shirt, she heard an elephant trumpet nearby. Another, higher pitched one followed.

'They've never had elephants here before!' she said to Khampa, and they walked quickly in the direction of the sound. They came upon a special section of the park's animal pens. In the back of the area, beating a bunch of hay against her wrinkled knee, was a large elephant, and peeking out from behind her massive legs was a hairy elephant calf. The mother elephant was showing her calf the proper

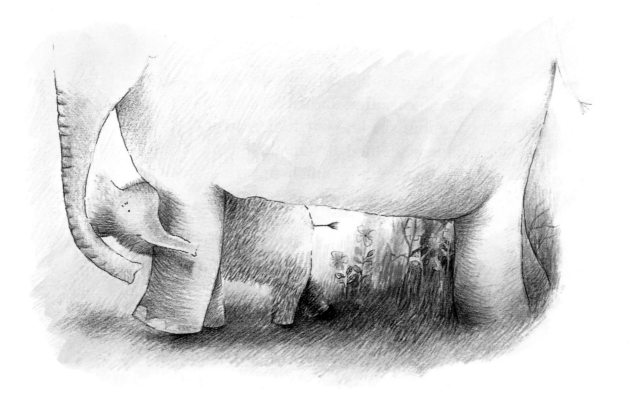

way to clean their food before eating.

Khampa kept his distance from the elephants; they smelt different from any animal he had seen before. As they beat the hay, the elephants also flapped their great floppy ears back and forth, like giant fans.

'There's an idea!' Meena said. 'They flap their ears to keep cool!'

She tried to flap her own ears, but it was not as easy as it looked. At first, nothing happened at all—she just squinted her eyes and thought about moving her ears. She tried so hard that her eyebrows began to wiggle up and down, but she knew that wasn't the same. She tried so hard that her head wagged side to side, but she knew that also wasn't the same. The elephants seemed to fan their ears so effortlessly, but no matter how much she tried, her ears would not move.

'I just can't do it!' she said in frustration. 'I'm not giving up, Khampa—one of these animals must have a way to get cool that will work for me too.'

As Meena and Khampa walked back down the narrow path, they heard splashing somewhere ahead. They followed the sound to a pool ringed by jagged stones. In the middle of the pool, a pair of ducks happily dunked their heads in the water and splashed themselves. Drops of water rolled down their feathers like clear marbles.

Meena sat quietly by the edge of the pool, looking into the water. The bottom was littered with crushed cans, empty bags of crisps, and old newspapers, all covered with slimy green algae.

'Khampa, I'd like to dive into the pond with these ducks, but it's so dirty … Wait!' she said, looking at Khampa. 'I've got an idea. Let's go home—quickly!'

Meena began to run through the park, back to her house. Khampa ran ahead. She opened the door to her house and called out to her mother, 'I've figured it out, Ma!'

'What are you talking about?' asked her mother from her study.

'You'll see!'

Her mother was busy working and decided to let Meena carry on doing whatever mischief she might be up to.

Meena went into the bathroom with Khampa and filled the bath with cool water.

'Here's the pool,' Meena said and slipped into the water.

Then she took two yellow rubber duckies from a

shelf and set them floating merrily in the water.

'And here are the ducks! There! A swim with the ducks … I think this is the best way to keep cool!'

Her mother, who had heard her splashing around in the tub and talking to Khampa, brought a nimbu-pani for her and a bowl of water for Khampa.

'Here's one more way,' she said, leaving Meena in the company of Khampa and the ducks.

Little and Things That Go Bump in the Night

SWAGATA DEB

Illustrated by Bindia Thapar

It was nearly midnight. Daddy, Mummy and Pickle had all gone to bed. Everyone was fast asleep, except for Little. Little sat waiting in front of her mother's mirror in the dressing room. She was waiting for her hair to grow.

In the morning, Little's hairdresser had given her a haircut. She had cut Little's hair really short. Just when Little was about to cry, Daddy had assured her that her hair would soon grow long and silky, and it would look just like Mummy's! (What he hadn't told her was that it would take the hair several years to grow that long. And that there would be many haircuts in between.)

Little was feeling very sleepy. So far, her hair showed no signs of growing. But she didn't want to be asleep when it happened. So she tried hard to keep her eyes open. If only TS, the cat, was awake, they could have played, but even TS was fast asleep.

The clock in the living room struck twelve. After the twelfth gong, Little suddenly heard strange noises coming from the living room next door. There was first a little creak, then a moan, then a GROAN. Then several creaks, several moans and several GROANS.

Little's sleepiness disappeared. She came out of the room to investigate.

Any other child in her place would have

been scared. But Little was different. She didn't believe in ghosts, and she was never scared. That was because every night, before going to bed, Daddy would tell Pickle and Little a ghost story. After the story, all three of them would laugh about it and go to sleep. When Little came into the living room, she did not see any ghosts or monsters or even thieves. Everything in the living room seemed just as it should be. Had she imagined the noises?

She looked around again, carefully this time. And she saw, to her astonishment, that all the furniture pieces in the room—the sofas, the chairs, the dining table, even the little footstools—were stretching and moving and muttering to themselves!

The big sofa called out to the small

sofa in a deep voice: 'Come on, it's time for our daily walk!'

One small sofa curled up and said in a small voice: 'Can't I rest just a bit more?'

Little did not know what to do. Should she stay hidden behind the curtain and watch secretly, or should she come forward and speak to her furniture? She decided to talk, because her mind

was full of questions and Little didn't like unanswered questions.

She came right up to the centre of the room, and held out her hand to the big sofa. 'Hello,' she said, 'I'm Little.'

'Of course, I know you,' said the big sofa in a friendly booming voice. 'You are the lightest and kindest. You don't jump up and down on my tummy like that Pickle does. And you don't scratch me, like TS.'

Little felt very curious. She asked the big sofa, 'Do all of you go for a walk every night?'

'Of course. We have to! Just think what our job is like. We lounge around all day in front of the TV, waiting for people to sit on us! At least I like watching TV and observing people. Otherwise, my job would be dreadfully boring. But even then, how much TV can one watch in a day, without getting fat and stupid and very unhealthy? No, we need exercise! Come on, now, Small Sofas, you lazy bums, hurry up!' The big sofa pushed the small sofas, and they started marching about the room. Little watched them with her mouth open in amazement.

The paintings climbed down the walls and walked to Mummy's dressing room. They took turns looking at themselves in the mirror. They brushed

69

their hair with Mummy's hairbrush, which grumbled: 'Hey, that hurts!' They used Mummy's lipsticks, and pirouetted and posed in front of the mirror, and admired themselves. Little stood silently behind them.

She heard one painting say to another: 'No matter how much we dress up, no one in the house notices us any more. But who cares? People who see us for the first time adore us. Isn't it wonderful being a painting?'

Little had had no idea that the paintings were so vain. She found it quite funny, but she knew that if she giggled, the beauties would be offended. So she kept quiet.

She heard a rattling sound. It seemed to be coming from the windows. The windows were calling her! She went to them and greeted them politely.

One of the windows said: 'Will you please paint a red cross or something on me? I like the way I am, but it's not good for my self-esteem. People are looking through me all the time.'

Little realized that this was true. People hardly ever noticed windows. They looked at other things through them. So she got her set of paints, and painted bright flowers on all the windows. The windows were delighted!

The doormat crept up to her and was clearing its throat, about to speak. She could well imagine what the poor thing had to say. She picked it up and dusted it well. She patted it very gently, and said she would see to it that people were not too rough with it.

'You are a very kind child,' said a voice behind her. It was the TV. 'Will you listen to my story?'

'Of course, I will,' said Little.

The TV began its tale of woe. 'No one has any time to listen to my story. Throughout the day, I am busy telling stories that other people have written and acted out. People use me to advertise their soaps and

shampoos and dog food and whatnot. But I never get a chance to tell my own story!'

'I'll listen to you,' said Little. 'Please tell me your story.' She had started feeling sorry for all of them. She could not think of them any more as just pieces

of furniture. People just used them and forgot about them. They never stopped to think that they might also have feelings.

The TV began its story. It told Little how it had been

 72

made in a factory along with hundreds of other TVs and how it was sent to a shop. It described how it came to Little's house, and how much it loved Little's family. 'I was born to give people a fun time,' the TV said. 'Making people happy gives me great joy. We are better than newspapers at covering news. Soon people will stop reading books and spend all their time watching us.'

'That's not a good thing, is it?' objected Little. 'Daddy was telling me the other day that I should watch less TV and read more books.'

The TV set was silent for a while. Little wondered if she shouldn't have said this. Was the TV sulking?

But when the TV spoke again, it didn't sound unhappy. 'I think we are great babysitters,' it said. 'Children love us. It's only the grown-ups who think that too much TV is bad for them.'

This was a completely new idea for Little. She thought about it in silence.

Suddenly, the music system began to play: *Desmond had a barrow in the marketplace ...*' The chairs and sofas linked their armrests and started dancing to the music. The rocking chair rocked.

The curtains fluttered. The lights grew dimmer and

73

brighter to the song's rhythm. There was a party in the living room!

Little went into the kitchen to see what was happening there. It was no longer as neat as Mummy left it every night!

The dishes had climbed out of the dish rack. The spoons had walked out of their drawer. There was something cooking in the pressure cooker. The teapot was busy pouring tea into all the cups. The vegetables had got out of the fridge and were walking about all over the floor. The eggs were all standing in a line. There was a tiny chicken among them. It looked like it had just hatched out of one of the eggs.

Little picked up a tomato and asked, 'What on earth is happening here?'

The tomato wriggled in her hand and said: 'We are about to begin the chicken-and-egg race.'

'But why are you having a chicken-and-egg race in the middle of the night?' asked Little.

The tomato patiently explained to her: 'People have never been able to figure out which came first, the egg or the chicken. So we are having this race tonight to settle the matter once and for all.'

Then the race began. The egg rolled along. The chicken flew a little, then hopped a little, then flew a little again. They were neck to neck.

The egg dashed against the wall at the end of the race, and broke. The floor was a mess. The vegetables standing near the finishing line got sprayed in egg yolk.

Mummy would have fainted if she had seen her kitchen at that moment, thought Little. Mummy kept the kitchen so spotlessly clean. Little wondered how it would get tidied up now.

She need not have worried. Soon the broom and the mop took over the kitchen and started cleaning up in a brisk and efficient manner.

Little had had enough. She went back to her room. She lay in bed thinking about all the things that she had seen and heard. She wondered whether Daddy, Mummy and Pickle would believe her when she told them her story next morning.

As she was dozing off, she felt herself swaying slightly. The bed was gently rocking Little to sleep.

Just Like Ravana's Brother

ARTHY MUTHANNA SINGH

Illustrated by Nitin Chawla

'He just won't get up, Mummy,' Riten complained, coming into the house. 'He's lying there, right in the middle of my racetrack in the garden.'

Riten's mother was very busy. She had to complete her chores for the party that night. Putting the final touches to the flower arrangement for the dining table, she murmured, 'Have your racetrack somewhere else, Riten.'

'I can't,' Riten cried, 'it's the only spot where my cars can fly over the drain like the Grand Prix drivers do.'

Riten was quite upset by now. He had already tried everything possible to wake that huge man. He ran to his mother and stood in her path. 'Mummy, listen to me properly. I have tried everything. I've even shouted into his ear.'

His mother said sternly, 'Please, Riten, I have so much more to do. Why don't you ask Kutty to help you?'

Riten walked slowly to Kutty's room, but couldn't find him. 'Kutty!' he shouted.

There was no reply. Riten was sure that Kutty had heard him and was either pretending not to have heard, or was hiding.

Tiptoeing into the kitchen, Riten swiftly checked behind the rice box, behind the screen and under the table. No sign of Kutty. Creeping into the dark veranda, he found Kutty fast asleep, curled up on the divan.

'Sleeping seems to be the favourite occupation here today,' he said loudly. And when there was still

no response, he put his mouth close to Kutty's ear and screamed!

Kutty jumped up, looking frightened. On seeing Riten, he became very angry. 'Why did you have to do that?' he yelled. 'I was having such a lovely, delicious dream.' He lay down again. 'Ice creams and halwa and so much kulfi! All for me!'

'Hey, wait, Kutty,' Riten interrupted, 'don't go back to sleep. I need your help.'

Kutty pushed Riten away. 'Go away, I'm busy. Come back later,' he said.

Riten tried to pull him up. 'Please, Kutty, listen to me. I promise to give you two kulfis if you help me.'

Kutty sat up immediately. 'How will you give me two kulfis?' he asked. 'You have no pocket money left.'

Riten reluctantly said, 'I'll give you my share of kulfis when Papa takes us out on Sunday.'

Kutty looked very pleased. Sunday was just two days away.

'Okay,' he said. 'Now, what's your problem? I hope it's a good one—good enough to lose my dream for.'

'Well,' began Riten, 'I was planning a race with all my cars. But I found this huge man sleeping right in the middle of my racetrack in the garden. I shouted at him, pushed him, tried to move him ... everything. But he is still happily snoring away!'

Kutty nodded his head very knowingly. 'Did he have a big tummy?' he asked.

'Yes,' said Riten, 'a huge, huge tummy!'

'Ah!' said Kutty wisely. 'He must be Kumbhakarna. All the signs and clues point to that.'

'Who? We'll have to find a way to wake him before the party at least,' said Riten, looking worried.

'Wouldn't the guests be really shocked to see that huge man sleeping in the middle of the garden?' Kutty burst out laughing at the thought.

Taking Riten's hand, he ran into the garden. The huge man was still asleep, snoring loudly.

Kutty suddenly let out a piercing yell.

There was no reaction, except from Pamela next door. 'I'm trying to study. Will you try and keep quiet?' she said angrily.

Kutty and Riten sat down on the lawn to think.

Suddenly, Kutty had the answer. 'Where's your firecracker collection, Riten?' he asked excitedly.

'Why?' asked Riten, puzzled. 'Diwali's still weeks away.'

'Don't waste any more time,' said Kutty, 'let's go.'

Riten took Kutty to the dark attic, where he had hidden his collection in three of their father's old shoeboxes, behind the wooden beam of the roof. Kutty quickly opened the boxes and glanced through the contents.

'Ah!' he exclaimed finally. 'This is going to be our weapon!' He held up a lethal-looking string of 'hydrogen' bombs—the loudest, most frightening firecracker of all.

'Are we going to burst these bombs now?' asked Riten.

'Sure,' said Kutty. 'If these bombs don't wake Mr K, nothing will. Come on.'

'But …' said Riten.

'What's the problem?' asked Kutty.

'Pamela will get angry again,' said Riten. 'She might complain to Mummy.'

'We can't help that. We'll explain to her later. We have to wake him up. Come on,' said Kutty firmly.

They picked up a box of matches from the kitchen and went out again. Mr K hadn't moved.

'Who is Kumbhakarna?' asked Riten.

'He was Ravana's brother,' said Kutty.

'I know Ravana, the rakshasa with a hundred heads!'

85

exclaimed Riten. 'But how can his brother be sleeping in our garden?'

'Kumbhakarna used to sleep for six months of the year, and to wake him up, a large band was needed to make loud noises. Lots of elephants too,' said Kutty wisely. 'He used to eat a lot too.'

'I see,' said Riten thoughtfully.

Kutty quickly placed the firecrackers on the ground,
lit the fuse and, pulling Riten with him, ran behind
the water tank.

'Close your ears,' he shouted.

Riten and Kutty sat with their hands over their ears.

A few minutes went by. Nothing happened.

Riten slowly removed his hands from over his ears. 'Maybe it's a bad bomb,' he said. 'Maybe …'

'Maybe it is too old,' said Kutty. Suddenly …

BOOOOOOOOOOOOOM! BOOOOOOOOOM! BOOOOOOOOOOOOM!

When everything was silent again, Riten and Kutty came out from their hiding spot. Mr K was stirring.

'Good, good! It worked!' cried Kutty with glee.

Mr K was rubbing his eyes now. Kutty and Riten watched him in great anticipation.

Mr K opened his eyes and saw the two boys. 'Where am I?' he asked feebly. 'Who are you?'

'Who are you?' asked Kutty. 'What are you doing here?'

The giant looked around him. He scratched his head. 'Er … I … I … I really don't know,' he said, finally. 'The last thing I remember was that I'd gone for a wedding feast and eaten a lot of good food. My sister said that I'd eaten too much. I'm very fond of food, you see. Especially sweets.'

'Me too,' said Kutty.

'Me too,' agreed Riten.

'I can't remember anything after that,' said Mr K sadly. 'Anyway, I had better go home now. I have to get ready to start another week of work tomorrow, after this lovely weekend.'

'Tomorrow? Weekend?' asked Kutty. 'But today is Friday.'

'WHAT?' Mr K jumped up and dusted the leaves off his clothes. 'But the wedding was on Sunday! I couldn't have slept for so many days!'

'Maybe you haven't got the dates right,' suggested Riten.

'No, no!' cried Mr K. 'I'm sure, because it was my sister's birthday— 7 March.'

Now it was the turn of Kutty and Riten to look surprised. 'But today is 8 September!'

'You must be joking!' said Mr K disbelievingly. 'I must go. Bye, boys. Sorry for the trouble.' He started running out.

'Hey!' shouted Kutty. 'What's your name?'

'My name? It's Kumbha ...' he started.

Kutty interrupted him. 'I knew it! I knew it!'

'...konam,' finished the man.

Riten burst out laughing!

'I was sure it would be something else,' said Kutty, looking slightly crestfallen.

Scaredy Cat

SAMPURNA CHATTARJI

Illustrated by Anitha Balachandran

The cat's name was Scaredy. Scaredy Cat.

He had no brothers, sisters, cousins, aunts or uncles.

All he had was a sneeze.

Or rather, the sneeze had him.

Whenever he saw the wheels grinding or the smoke blowing or the lights flashing, the sneeze took him by the neck and shook him.

Aaaaaaaaachhhhhhhooooooo!

His eyes watered. His nose ran. His paws twitched. His claws itched.

And the little children saw him and said: Scaredycat Scaredycat.

And that's how he knew his name.

It can get lonely when all you've got in the whole wide world is a sneeze.

He closed his eyes and thought.

Dark. Black. Scaredy.

Big. Brown. Scaredy.

Sharp. Stone. Scaredy.

Up. Down. Scaredy.

Voice. Loud. Scaredy.

Wheels. Fast. Scaredy.

Feet. Many. Scaredy.

Blinding. Lights. Scaredy.

If all these things are scaredy, then what am I?

And if I'm scaredy, then what are these?

And if either is neither, then which is what?

Tired after all this thinking, he fell asleep.

It was night when he woke.

Dark black night.

Big brown shapes.

Many fast feet.

Blinding lights.

Rushing wheels.

Shouting voices.

He was sitting on top of a big tin drum.

On the other side of the drum were the railway tracks.

Quiet.

Shh.

Then suddenly—

Whoooooooosssh!

A big black snake rushed past.

It thundered.

It shuddered.

It had bright-yellow eyes all along its side.

The eyes were full of shapes.

Men, women.

They hung from the eyes like tears.

The air was full of sound and light.

And then it was quiet again.

Shh.

Ten whole minutes passed before he realized.

He hadn't sneezed.

He had been so busy looking he had forgotten about the sneeze.

Or rather the sneeze had forgotten about him.

His paws didn't twitch.

His claws didn't itch.

His nose didn't run.

Only his eyes. His eyes watered.

He was crying for the shapes he had seen.

He was crying for not having seen them sooner.

He was crying because he was no longer afraid.

Scaredy had sat in the train and gone.

Cat was left. All alone.

Even the sneeze had gone and left him.

All that remained was the

twinkling windows in the sky, the

happy voices in the street, the

running wheels, the

flashing lights, the

shiny bright towers and the

little children saying:

Scaredycat Scaredycat,

all because he was crying.

For joy.

Very Good Turbans

ASHA NEHEMIAH

Illustrated by Loveleen Chawla

V.G. Thallappa had the best turban shop in town. He had all sorts of turbans—tall turbans with feathers and small turbans with flowers. There were soft turbans made of silk and satin, and stiff turbans made of silver lace and gold ribbons. Every turban in the shop had been made by V.G. Thallappa.

One day, Thallappa said to his son, 'Gopu, please look after the shop. I am going to buy some pink muslin to make turbans.'

Gopu was playing outside. He came into the shop bouncing his big ball.

'Father,' he said, 'I do not know how to make turbans. What will I do if someone comes into the shop and asks me to make a new turban for him?'

'Don't worry, son,' V.G. Thallappa said, 'There are enough turbans kept ready in my shop to fit every kind of head. No one will ask you to make a new

turban.' He set off with his big bag, leaving Gopu alone in the shop.

In a few minutes, the door of the shop opened. In walked the biggest, tallest, largest man Gopu had ever seen.

'Oh no,' thought Gopu, looking at the size of the man's head, 'there's not a single turban in my father's shop that will fit this man.'

'Hello, V.G. Thallappa,' said the big man loudly. He looked at Gopu closely. 'You look rather short and small to me, but that may be because I'm not wearing my spectacles. My friends tell me you are called VGT because you make Very Good Turbans.'

'Yes,' said Gopu.

'I'm getting married tomorrow. I want you to make me the best turban in the world. The turban should be so grand that everyone at the wedding will look at me and only me.'

Gopu didn't know what to do. There were two shelves full of silver wedding turbans and one shelf full of golden wedding turbans, but none of them would fit the big man's big head.

'Hurry up!' shouted the big man. 'If you don't make

me a grand turban at once, I will change your name to VBT—Very Bad Turbans.'

Gopu was very worried. He didn't want anyone to call his father Very Bad. He picked up a piece of orange silk and twisted it this way and that way. And then he turned it round and round and round. But it did not look like a turban. It looked like an orange bird's nest.

Gopu tried a length of purple cotton. He twirled it this way and that way, and round and round and round. But it did not look like a turban either. It looked like a large purple egg.

Gopu looked at his big ball. He had an idea.

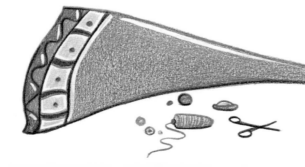

He took a sharp knife and cut his ball into two. The two halves were like two big caps, which were large enough to fit the big man's head. He felt very sad to cut up his ball, but there was nothing else he could do.

Gopi took one half of the ball and stuck some blue peacock feathers on it. Next, he wrapped a bit of silver ribbon around it. It looked good, but he thought it needed some more colour. So he fixed a bit of gold lace, many twirly sea shells, three strings of pearls and some shiny red stones on the ball. He topped it with a huge, shiny green tassel.

'How is this?' Gopu asked the large man, putting the new turban on the big man's head.

'Hmm,' said the big man looking into the mirror, 'I can't see very well without my spectacles, but your turban does fit me very well. Yes, it's very nice indeed. Tell me, do you think I will look so dashing that everyone at my wedding will look only at me?'

'Yes,' Gopu said with a smile. 'I'm quite sure everyone will look only at you.'

'Thank you, Very Good Thallappa,' said the big man, giving Gopu a big bundle of notes. He walked happily out of the shop.

The big man had a good reason to feel happy. All through his wedding, everyone looked at him and only him.

Breakfast

SAMIT BASU

Illustrated by Taposhi Ghoshal

It may be the most important meal of the day
But I'm just NOT having breakfast! No way!
I can't eat the same thing every day any more!
I hate breakfast! Breakfast's a bore!

My mother smiled and said, 'Well, dear,
You need to know more about breakfast, it's clear.
So why don't you travel around the world and see
What you would like your breakfast to be?'

So I packed my trunk and prepared for a feast!
I thought I would start in Japan, in the East,
I went there one morning and it was so nice …
I had miso soup and hot, steaming rice.

Then I went to China and had porridge (chou),
Pickles (sien tsai) and steamed bread (man tou),
This is delicious! I thought as I ate,
I sat on the Great Wall and the view was great!

I went to India next, and in Mumbai
There was so much colour I shut one eye!
There were so many different kinds of Indian food!
I chose idli and chutney, and it was very good…

I travelled up the sea to Turkey's shore
I'd had many breakfasts, but I wanted more!
Feta cheese, olives and white bread—I gobbled up
And drank hot apple tea in a special cup.

I packed my bags and went to France
(Wouldn't you if you had the chance?)
I ate a fresh, hot croissant with butter and jam
And drank hot chocolate—how lucky I am!

I'd tasted so many things; now I was in the mood
For some good plain solid British food.
So I walked to Scotland on my own strong legs
And ate haggis, kippers, bacon and eggs.

I crossed the Atlantic Ocean on a ship
And went to Jamaica, licking my lips!
Eggs, tomatoes and flying fish for me—
With toast and jam and Caribbean coffee!

I'd eaten many breakfasts, but I was hungry still.
So I went south and danced the samba in Brazil!
I ate acai, a fruit from the Amazon's trees.
And pao de queijo, bread made of cheese.

Who knew breakfast could be such a lovely treat?
As I went to Mexico I thought, what will I eat?
It was easy! Eggs with corn tortillas of course,
With beans in a delicious spicy tomato sauce.

I stopped by in the US for a cereal treat
And waffles and maple syrup, warm and sweet.
How could I have not liked breakfast, I wonder.
Which one's the best, I plod as I ponder.

And thought all the way from Rio to Rome
And then I thought—I miss the breakfast at home!
It's great to travel and eat what you find
But the very best food is what you leave behind!

So I ran home to Mother, who already knew
What I'd want for breakfast—you should try it too!
Grass, mangoes, leaves and bark from a young tree,
Is the best food for a growing elephant like me!

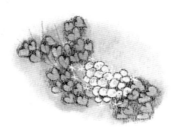

The Ice Berries

STEPHEN AITKEN AND SYLVIA SIKUNDAR

Illustrated by Ajanta Guhathakurta

Usha's home was high up in the Himalayas. It was very beautiful but life was not easy for Usha and her family. They grew a few vegetables and kept several yaks which gave them milk and wool. Her father was a guide, and he would go away for months at a time.

Usha and her brother would take it in turns every morning to take the yaks to find fresh grass. The person who stayed at home would look after their old grandfather.

One monsoon day, it was Usha's turn. Late in the afternoon, a wild storm blew in. Deep-purple clouds floated overhead in an angry sky like giant inkdrops. Usha struggled to gather her yaks together. 'Come on! Come on!' she yelled as large cold raindrops splashed off her head and hands.

Suddenly, Usha slipped on the wet stones. She rolled and tumbled down the mountainside until a large rock stopped her fall. She lay there unconscious and still.

The storm rumbled and rolled through the mountains for several hours but then it was gone. Jupiter rose in the east and a full moon peeked over the mountaintops.

Usha woke up shivering in the chilly night air. She sat up and looked around. In the misty moonlight she could see the icy blue outline of one yak peering down at her. It was Chandu, named after the moon.

'What happened? Where am I?' Usha murmured. She got to her feet and stumbled towards the yak. As she grabbed his long wet hair to keep her balance, Chandu lowered his head and knelt down. Somehow, Usha climbed on his back and slumped over. The yak followed the long moonlit path home over the rolling hills.

Rajesh ran up the path to meet her. 'What happened? We were so worried when you didn't come home at sunset,' he cried, helping her down from the yak. 'We searched everywhere for you.'

'I fell and hit my head. When I woke up, Chandu was waiting beside me. He carried me home.' Usha hugged her yak.

From that night onwards, Usha and Chandu were inseparable. Wherever she went, the yak was always close behind.

One morning, Usha found Chandu lying on the ground. 'Get up, Chandu!' she said. 'It's time to go!'

Chandu rolled over and let out a moan.

'Grandfather! Grandfather!' called Usha. 'Come quickly! Chandu is sick.'

Her grandfather hobbled out of the house and knelt down beside the yak. He shook his head. 'Chandu is not well. We don't have any medicine to cure him but he may recover if we keep him warm and let him rest.'

'Stay with Chandu,' said Rajesh when he saw Usha crying. 'I'll take care of the other yaks.'

All that day Usha sat beside Chandu. 'Get better, Chandu, please get better,' she whispered over and over as she stroked his brown furry head. But the yak grew weaker and weaker. She gave him water to drink and tasty sweets to eat but he took no notice.

The golden sun set behind the snow-capped peaks. Rajesh came home and tethered the yaks outside the house. At the same time, a monk wearing ochre robes came along the path.

Grandfather greeted him, 'Please sit and drink tea.'

It was the custom in the mountains to give shelter to travellers. As Usha prepared strong tea with salt and yak butter, she couldn't hold back her tears.

'What's wrong?' asked the monk as Usha placed the glass of hot tea on the table beside him.

'Chandu, my yak, is sick and we don't have any medicine to cure him,' she sobbed.

'Let me see him,' said the monk.

The monk went into the shed and stroked the yak's

head. 'There is only one thing that can save him. He needs wild ice berries which grow high on the mountain peaks. They are difficult to find, but they will make him better.'

'None of us can travel that far,' said Grandfather. 'My old legs will not carry me up the steep mountain paths. My son, Bahadur, won't be home for several weeks.'

'Grandfather! Let me go,' said Usha.

The old man shook his head. 'It's too dangerous for you. Storms come suddenly. People say a yeti lives up there and many travellers have disappeared mysteriously.'

'Grandfather, have you ever seen a yeti?' asked Usha.

'No, but I've heard many stories,' said the old man, stroking his long grey beard thoughtfully.

'I don't believe in yetis,' said Usha with a shrug.

Early next morning, Chandu was still very sick. Usha packed some flat brown bread, yak milk cheese and tulsi leaves in her basket. She called Rajesh and whispered to him, 'I am going to find the ice berries.'

'But it is dangerous in the high mountains,' said Rajesh.

'I'll be back by evening,' said Usha. 'I promise.'

She set off at a brisk pace towards the peaks. It is hot in the mountains when the sun shines. The sun beat down and Usha stumbled several times on the steep

path. Each time, she picked herself up and kept climbing. She travelled through the rhododendron forests, the trees laden with crimson flowers shone in the morning light.

At midday, Usha reached the snowline. She sat in the snow, too short of breath to take another step.

Suddenly, a deep rumbling sound echoed across the silent snow. It came in waves followed by deep silence. 'Ommm, Ommm, Ommm.'

Usha jumped up and looked around for a place to hide. She saw a cave and crept inside. It was dark and damp.

117

'Ommm, Ommm, Ommm.'

Oh no! The sound came from somewhere close by. Usha peered into the gloom and saw the outline of a large hairy animal.

'It's the yeti,' she whispered.

The yeti whimpered and slowly raised his foot.

'You're injured,' said Usha. She forgot her grandfather's warning and went towards the yeti. 'I have some tulsi leaves in my bag; they will help your foot heal.'

The yeti winced when Usha wrapped the healing leaves around his foot.

'I need something to keep the leaves in place.' She looked around, but the dark, damp cave was bare. She took her woollen shawl off her shoulders, tore it into strips and wrapped it around the tulsi leaves.

'Your leg will get better soon,' she said. 'Now I must go and find wild ice berries for my yak, Chandu. He is very sick.'

The yeti stirred. He stretched and uncurled until his head almost touched the roof of the cave. For a moment Usha felt frightened as the yeti towered above her. But he touched her hand gently, limped out of the cave and beckoned Usha to follow.

Although he moved slowly, Usha had to scramble over the rocks to keep up. When they came to a dark, narrow ravine in the mountains, Usha hesitated as a cold breeze blew over her head and face. Just ahead she saw a gate covered in ice. The yeti tried to open it, but the gate was frozen shut.

The yeti stepped over the gate. He turned around and lifted Usha over the gate.

They walked past tiny waterfalls which tinkled like wind chimes and splashed over turquoise rocks into silver pools.

'A secret garden,' said Usha. 'I could never have found this by myself.'

The yeti shuffled along a path of white velvet snow and stopped by a cluster of icy blue vines. He searched through the heart-shaped leaves until he found clusters of crystal berries sparkling like tiny rainbows.

'Ice berries!' cried Usha.

She picked some of the berries, wrapped them in vine leaves and put them into her basket. Then she followed the yeti's footprints as they walked back out of the garden.

When they reached the yeti's cave, Usha gave him the bread and yak milk cheese.

'Thank you for helping me find the ice berries. My Chandu now has a chance to get better.' She touched the yeti's hand to say goodbye and saw tears in his eyes. 'Don't be sad. Now that I know

where you live, I'll come and visit you again.'

She walked carefully down the steep mountain path because she didn't want to fall again. As night fell, she could see strange shadows dancing on the rocks and hear muffled whisperings. Finally, she reached the path near her home and saw the tiny lights of her house. A dim yellow light was coming closer and closer as it bobbed up and down.

She heard Rajesh's voice. 'Usha! Usha! Is that you?' She ran down the path to meet him.

'You're safe,' said Rajesh, hugging her close. 'I was afraid that you had met the yeti.'

'I did meet the yeti,' replied Usha as they walked home.

Grandfather was waiting for them. 'Usha! You're safe! I was so worried about you,' he said, holding her face in his weathered hands.

'I'm sorry, Grandfather,' said Usha. 'But I had to try to save Chandu. I've brought the ice berries.'

She ran straight to Chandu who was lying on a blanket in the shed. She sat on the floor beside the yak and opened the vine leaves.

The berries had melted. Usha saw the soggy leaves and burst into tears. Chandu raised his head and licked the moisture off the leaves. Then he turned towards Usha and licked the tears from her cheeks. He rolled over again and lay still.

After a few moments, Chandu slowly stood on all four wobbly legs.

'Chandu, you're getting better!' Usha threw her arms around the yak's neck.

'You're lucky you didn't meet the yeti up on the mountain,' said Grandfather.

'I did meet him,' said Usha. 'He showed me where the ice berries grow.'

'I thought you didn't believe in yetis,' said Grandfather.

'I do now,' replied Usha.

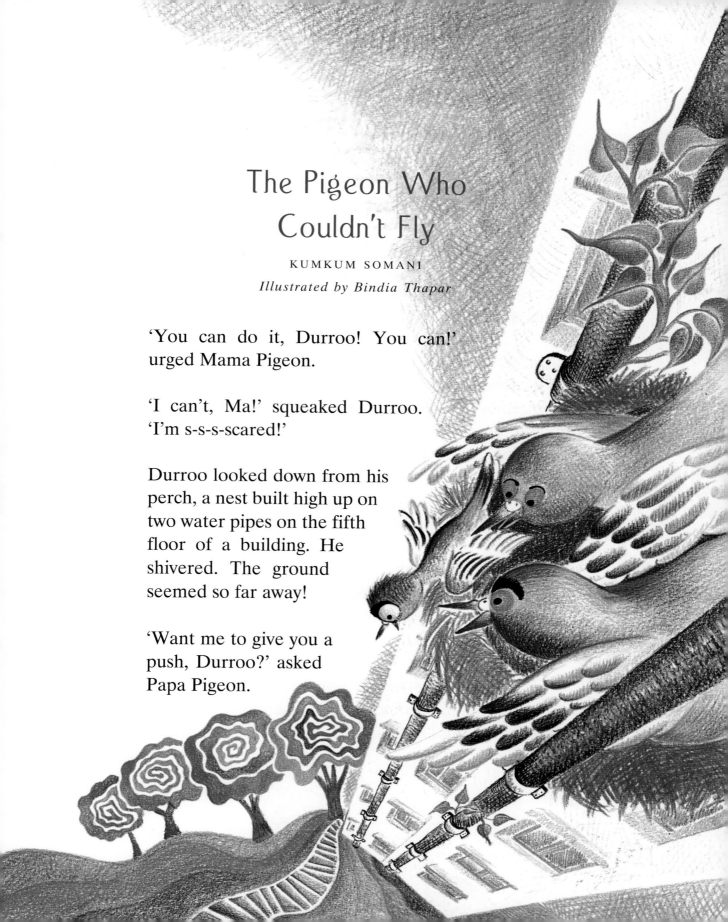

The Pigeon Who Couldn't Fly

KUMKUM SOMANI

Illustrated by Bindia Thapar

'You can do it, Durroo! You can!' urged Mama Pigeon.

'I can't, Ma!' squeaked Durroo. 'I'm s-s-s-scared!'

Durroo looked down from his perch, a nest built high up on two water pipes on the fifth floor of a building. He shivered. The ground seemed so far away!

'Want me to give you a push, Durroo?' asked Papa Pigeon.

'N-n-no, Pa!' said Durroo. 'I want to try flying on my own.'

This was on a Monday.

Tuesday, Wednesday and Thursday went by. On Friday morning, Mama Pigeon said, 'Durroo, all your friends on the neem tree were born at the same time as you. They are flying. Why aren't you?'

'Ma,' Durroo had his arguments ready, 'when you start flying, you tire easily. You need to rest on something. My friends from the neem tree have so many branches to rest on. What do I have? Nothing!' He began to cry.

'Now he's blaming us for building our nest on top of these pipes on the fifth floor!' said Mama.

'We chose this high spot because we thought you and Manu, your little brother, would be safe from cats, rats, lizards and snakes who love eating baby pigeons,' said Papa.

'Your wings are stronger now,' said Popo, the old parrot who had come to visit the pigeon family. 'Give it a shot, Durroo! You won't fall, I promise.'

'That's easy for you to say,' said Durroo rudely. 'If I fall, I'll die. Not you!'

'Leave him be,' said Mama. 'His baby brother will grow up and teach him to fly!'

Durroo went away and sulked. He badly wanted to be a hero to Manu, but Manu seemed so much smarter than him. Now he would even start flying before he did.

That night, Durroo dreamt his father gave him a push and he tumbled out of his nest.

But his wings refused to open!

Luckily, Popo saw him falling. He popped a parachute in Durroo's beak. The parachute opened … and … *phew* … Durroo was saved!

Popo and Durroo then sailed away blissfully to the neem tree. There they met sparrows, crows, bulbuls, mynahs, eagles, sunbirds and, of course, pigeons, and they all had on neat little parachutes!

What fun!

'It's Rest Day for our wings, Durroo,' they chanted. 'Come, sail with us to Cloud 9!'

Then, Durroo woke up.

His family heard him shout: 'Parachute! I want a parachute for my birthday!'

Durroo told Manu his dream when his parents had gone to gather food.

'Is it so difficult to fly?' asked Manu.

'Maybe not,' sighed Durroo. 'Maybe I'm just a scaredy puss!'

'You're not,' said Manu loyally. 'You are the nicest brother in the whole world.'

'But what shall I do?' asked Durroo. 'I want to fly, but every time I look down, it is so far away that I get scared.'

'Well,' said Manu thoughtfully, 'let's try looking

down first without getting scared. Then we can move to flying.'

The two brothers looked down. They saw a grey blob climbing up their pipe.

'Looks like a rat,' said Durroo.

'A rat with sharp, yellow teeth.'

The grey blob came nearer and grinned wickedly. 'Hi, birds,' he leered. 'I'm Rat-a-tat. I am a rat.'

'Hi,' said Durroo. 'I'm Durroo and he's Manu. We are pigeons.'

'I know!' said Rat-a-tat. 'I have been watching both of you since you were born. And your parents love you, for they have fed you well!'

'Have you come to play with us?' asked Manu, who, though he was very smart, did not know too many other kinds of creatures.

'But, of course,' grinned the rat. 'I know a great game! I'll nibble at your wings, and you'll feel ticklish. You'll laugh. Then I'll nibble at your claws, your neck, your …' The rat's mouth was watering.

Durroo was not as smart as Manu, but he was older after all. He remembered something Papa had said the previous day … 'We built our nest so high so you would be safe from cats, rats, lizards and snakes …'

RAT-A-TAT WAS A RAT!

How ugly his eyes looked! How wicked his yellow teeth! How scary his twitching whiskers!

Durroo flapped his wings feebly. 'Get out, you horrible beast!' he shouted.

He saw Popo flying past. 'Popo! Help! Help!' he squawked.

'Hold fort, Durroo,' shouted Popo. He knew alone he was no match for the rat. 'I'll get my neem-tree friends to save you both.'

'He'll be too late!' snarled Rat-a-tat, lunging at Manu, who was trying to climb out of the nest on to the pipes on which it rested.

Durroo flapped his wings feebly and tried to peck Rat-a-tat. But the rat had already clawed at Manu. Drops of blood fell on the pipes. Poor little Manu looked terrified.

Durroo saw red. 'Don't touch my brother!' he screeched as he hopped towards the rat.

'Look down, Durroo,' urged the rat slyly from where he was climbing on the pipes. 'The ground is far below. Remember, you can't fly.'

'I can't fly.' The old fear welled up again inside Durroo. 'How will I stop him if I can't fly?' he thought.

'I won't look down!' sobbed Durroo. 'I'm s-s-s-scared!'

The rat laughed a horrible squeaky laugh. His ugly, yellow teeth were very, very near. He lunged at Manu again and just missed, as Manu slithered back as far as he could go.

A wave of anger swept over Durroo. 'I will save Manu even if I have to die!' he screeched. Without looking down, or thinking any more, he threw himself on the rat.

'Glug!' screamed the rat, thrown off balance by this unexpected attack.

And Durroo? Surprisingly he was still afloat! He flapped his wings. They were quite strong! He flapped them again. He was flying! He charged at the rat with all his might.

'Let's make a deal,' said the crafty rat, clinging to the pipes. 'Give me the baby! I won't bother you!'

'Shut up!' Durroo struck the rat's face with his wings again and again.

'Help!' screamed the rat, swinging from the pipe.

Durroo's beak poked the rat's eye. And the rat let go.

Down, down, down, he fell. There was a loud thud. Then silence.

Suddenly, the air was filled with the squawking of many birds—bulbuls, parrots, sparrows, pigeons, crows, eagles, swallows and many others.

'We came to help you, Durroo! But you don't need our help! You can fly!'

'You saved your little brother!' This was Papa. He looked proudly at his son.

The birds squawked and cheered as Mama Pigeon gave her brave boy a peck on his feathery cheek.

'You're my hero!' smiled Manu, hugging him.

The House That Never Stayed Home

ANITA VACHHARAJANI

Illustrated by Anitha Balachandran

I liked spending my summer holidays with Grandpa and Grandma. They lived in an old house on top of a beautiful hill in Nainital. The house had a shiny red roof that glowed like a ruby in the sun. It was full of little corners and nooks where I could hide when Grandma wanted me to finish my holiday homework!

Every evening, Grandpa would sit on the swing outside with a plateful of mangoes. I would sit by him, listening to his stories about the trees and the mountains. Grandpa had a big, round tummy and a large moustache which curled up.

One evening, I asked him, 'Grandpa, why is our house so high up on the hill? It looks like it might fall down.'

Grandpa ate a slice of mango and wiped the drops of yellow juice off his moustache. 'Hrrr-hmph!' he said in his rumbly way. 'It's a long story…'

'A story! Tell me! Tell me!'

'Long, long ago, when I was a boy, my mother and I lived in a little house in a village far away …'

'Were you as small as me?' I asked.

'Yes, I was just as small as you. One night, we woke up hearing a loud *DHABAAAD-DHOOM!* It had rained so hard that our roof broke! So we had to find a new house to live in. We saw many houses— small, big, tall, short, fat and thin houses. But we didn't like any of them—till we found this one. It stood outside the woods. It wasn't too big or too small. It didn't have a leaky roof or a creaky floor. It had big, bright windows and a warm, wooden floor. We peeped in and saw that there was no one inside. So we took all our things and went right in. You like it too, don't you?'

'Oh yes, Grandpa!' I replied.

'Ah … But you don't know the secret of this house.'

'What secret?' I asked.

'Hmm, listen … There was a little yard in front and our cow Gangu stood there munching grass all day. The woods had tall trees and I climbed them all. From the treetops, I could see tiny animals and people walking around in the village far away. We went to the village once a week, and ate roasted peanuts …'

Grandpa's eyes looked dreamy—like he was going to fall asleep! So I poked a finger in his stomach and said, 'Grandpa! What happened then?'

Grandpa smiled down at me and replied, 'Oh-hrrrm! Yes, about a week later, I woke up one morning and looked out of the window to check if Gangu was all right—I did that every day. What do you think I saw?'

'Gangu?'

'No Gangu! Just lots of camels! And there were no trees around us—just lots and lots of sand. I woke Amma up and we ran out of the door looking for Gangu. A warm breeze blew and we had sand in our ears, noses and eyes! There were lots of brightly dressed people around us with camels and tents. We were in a desert! How had we got there? Some people stood outside our gate—they were surprised to see us too! Our house had appeared like magic that morning!'

'And what did you do then?'

'Well, Amma was sad about losing Gangu, but I was happy because I had new friends to play with. The children taught me some great games. We ate dates and ran on the sand dunes all day. Amma made friends with the women. They taught her how to make wonderful buttermilk. All our clothes were winter woollies, so we got hot and itchy until the women gave us some of their colourful clothes to wear …'

'Did you stay there forever?'

'Well, some days later, we woke up smelling something in the air—like rotting fish. We could hear a loud *whoosh-whoosh* sound. We ran and looked out of the window. And what do you think we saw?'

'Camels?'

'No, just lots and lots of water, and some tall coconut trees! I ran out of the house. We were on an island in the sea!'

'Oooh! What did your Amma say to that?'

'Amma was very sad—she hated the fishy smell! And all around us women were drying fish. We were frightened too because our house kept dashing around like that … And I missed my friends. But I

made some more on the island and we played in the water all day. I learnt how to swim and catch fish! There were turtles and big colourful sea shells everywhere. It was fun to lie on the sand, to listen to the *whoosh* of the bright-blue sea, and to watch the clouds float by. I found Amma coconuts and birds' eggs to eat because she didn't like fish. At night the children slept on the beach. But I had to stay indoors because Amma was scared the house would run off again!'

'Did you stay there forever?'

'Well, I tried to! When Amma wasn't looking, I went to each wall of the house and whispered to it that we could stay on the island forever! But what do you think happened?' Grandpa stopped to eat another piece of mango. He ate slowly.

I got impatient. 'Grandpa, don't stop now! Tell me!'

He wiped his moustache and said, 'Three or four days later, I woke up one morning hearing a loud *clacketty-clack!* I looked at Amma and saw that her teeth were chattering. I tried to say something but I could only hear more clacketty-clacking. My teeth were chattering too! It was freezing cold! We shivered and huddled together under our blankets!'

'Where were you, Grandpa? At the North Pole?'

'I don't know! A chill wind blew snowflakes in through cracks in the door. We were hungry and cold ...'

'And then ...?'

'Suddenly, we heard a loud *DHU-DOOM!* A window flew open and the snow rushed right in. An old woman pushed her head in through the snow and smiled at us. Then the rest of her climbed in. She was plump and short, with a large broomstick in her hand. Her bright-red hair was tied up in little plaits with yellow ribbons. Behind her we could see only snow—everything was shiny white.

"'Wh-who are you?" asked Amma. But the old woman just stood there huffing and puffing.

"'*Phooof, fooff* ... I'm Bullo Bi," she replied when at last she'd caught her breath. "I'm ... *puff* ... a witch.'"

'Weren't you scared, Grandpa?'

'Yes, I was! I'd heard that witches ate little boys, so I ran and hid behind a chair.

'Bullo Bi said, "I used to live in this naughty little house till it ran away one day!"

"'Oooh!" said Amma. "I knew there was something wrong! It's taken us all over the world! It is a naughty house!"

'Bullo Bi whispered, "Yes, and I've come to tell you the secret of this house..."

'Amma whispered back, "What secret?"

"'You see," said Bullo Bi, looking around, "this house can fly! And it doesn't like to stay at home!"

"'Yes!" said Amma nodding her head eagerly. "We know that! But how does it fly?"

'Bullo Bi sighed. "I have to fly around the world a lot because I am a witch and my work takes me to many places. But I hate flying on my broomstick because it gets so cold! So I put a spell on this house and when I wanted to go somewhere, it would fly there."

"'And then the house flew away from you?" said Amma.

"'Oh yes," said Bullo Bi. "One morning when I was out, it flew off on its own! So I had to find myself another house."

"'How did you find us?" I asked, coming out slowly from behind the chair.

'Bullo Bi said, "Last night, as I was flying across the sky, I saw the house dashing by. So I followed it here!"

"'Er …" said Amma. "We didn't know it was your house. You can have it back."

"'No, thank you!" said Bullo Bi, shaking her head so hard that her plaits flew around her head. "I have a new house that's not naughty at all. I just came to help you."

'"Well, we like the house, but how do we make it stay still?" Amma asked.

'Bullo Bi replied, "I could take you and the house back to Nainital where I live these days. I'll keep an eye on it. It won't run away with me watching it all day."

'"Oh thank you!" said Amma.

'Then Bullo Bi asked Amma for a long, strong rope. She tied one end of the rope to her broomstick and wound the rest around the house. We sat on the bed, holding on for dear life.

'Bullo Bi got on to her broom and yelled, "All set?"

'"Ye-yes!" we called out.

'And then with a mighty *zwoop*, Bullo Bi took off into the air! And behind her, the house was pulled up and away into the sky. *Swooosh*, we went! Over trees and hills and seas. We flew past birds and right through clouds! And landed here on this beautiful hill. I think the house liked Nainital so much, it never flew off again!'

When Grandpa finished his story, he leaned back and ate another slice of mango. I just stared at him—a flying house! Why, we could go anywhere in the world!

'Grandpa,' I whispered, 'can the house still fly?'

'Oh, I don't know. Why don't you find out?' said Grandpa with a twinkle in his eye.

I spent the rest of my vacation showing the house pictures of the world from one of Grandpa's big old books. I sat next to a different wall every day and told it all about the animals and trees and mountains of the world. I even showed it pictures of the moon!

Every morning, I would rush to the window to see if we had landed in Timbuktu or at the North Pole or in the Thar Desert. But the house never went anywhere! It just stayed home all day!

Grandpa smiled and winked every time he saw me looking out the window … I wonder why!

Scared Yet?

SAMIT BASU

Illustrated by Anitha Balachandran

Midnight. I was fast asleep and was dreaming
Of flying in night skies, my eyes bright and gleaming,

When back in my bedroom, a thunderous thump
Woke me up. I switched on the light. And I jumped.

A weird little monster lay flat by my bed—
Ears stuck out like great wings from his green head.

A sign on his tail read 'Kids scream when I roar!'
He'd tripped on my toy train, *ker-splat!* on the floor.

He bounced up and said, 'Ha! Tremble in fear!'
'I'm not scared,' I said, 'but why are you here?'

'Rubbish!' he cried, 'I see you a-shivering!
Your heart is a-thumping! Your legs are a-quivering!

Your teeth are a-chattering! Your stomach is jelly!'
'I'm NOT scared,' I said. 'You're just small and
  smelly.'

'Why aren't you scared?' he cried. I said, 'Don't stress,
But we modern kids are real tough to impress.

We've seen all the movies. We've heard all the stories.
We've played video games far more violent and gory

Than anything you could dream up.' 'That's not true!'
'It is! I've seen movies where monsters like you

Have to quit scaring children and start acting funny!
So go get a costume and start being a bunny!

You think you're scary? Please! Give me a break!

You have no idea how much I have to take!

Homework! Peer pressure! Insane competitions!
Music class! Karate! Career decisions!

Each day of the week I meet at least six teachers!
You think I'd be scared by little green creatures?'

'Please stop, I beg you,' he said. 'Or my ears
Will burn and explode! I'm fighting back tears!

So young! So angry! And in so much pain!
Sorry I disturbed you! Won't happen again!'

Right then, he decided to call it a day
He jumped to my window and *zoom!* flew away.

I giggled and lay back. Poor thing, I'd been rough.
Yes, I have problems, but life ain't that tough.

I've food in my stomach, a strong roof above me,
Friends, dreams, ambitions, and parents who love me.

I will climb my mountains, no matter how steep.
Okay, lecture over, I'm going back to sleep.

The Tiger Who Sucked His Paw

INCHOW

Illustrated by Agantuk

Deep in the forests of the Sunderbans, late one evening, Baghu the tiger cub was trying hard to fall asleep. On his left, his mother was snoring softly. His father was on the prowl somewhere.

Baghu snuggled into the warmth of his mother's fur. She stirred in her sleep. Baghu watched her closely.

When he was quite sure that she was not about to wake up, Baghu quietly slipped his left paw into his mouth and fell fast asleep.

Baghu awoke to find his father growling and gnashing his teeth. 'Just took at him! Whoever heard of a tiger cub who sucks his paw? At this rate, he will grow up to be a pussy cat.'

'I've tried scolding him, smacking him, starving him—nothing works! The other day—when you brought back that goat from your hunt—I even dipped his paw in bitter bile. But he just went and washed it off. I don't know what to do!' his mother groaned.

Baghu quickly rubbed his paw on the grass and stretched himself. He was very hungry.

'Let's have a look at that paw.' His father held Baghu's tiny paw in his own huge one and turned it around. 'It's wet, sticky and stinky! And even the nails are going soft! It doesn't even look like a tiger's paw any more,' he declared in disgust. 'No dinner for him until he learns to be a tiger!'

And Baghu was sent back to bed.

That night, when both his parents were out hunting, Baghu went to visit his old friend, Madam Alligator. She was always willing to listen to his complaints. Baghu told her the whole story. 'I don't see why I can't suck my paw,' he said huffily. 'After all, it is mine!'

'Poor Baghu!' said Madam Alligator. 'Well, I know a place where you can find lots of friends and where you can suck your paws as much as you like. But I am not sure whether you will like it there.'

'Of course, I will!' said Baghu, excited. 'Please, please, please, will you take me there?'

Baghu jumped on to her rough and bumpy back. They shuffled through the long grass and wobbled down to the creek. Madam Alligator splattered into the water.

Baghu looked up at the sky. There were a thousand stars and a full moon. Baghu sniffed. The wet, salty breeze smelt of fish.

Baghu and Madam Alligator drifted on the water all night. They came to an island just as dawn was breaking. 'This is the Island of the Wet Paws,' said Madam Alligator.

When Baghu landed on the shore, many creatures came romping up on their hind legs. They were all furiously sucking their two front paws. 'Ueollugh! Geullough!' they said in welcome.

Baghu was filled with joy, though he could not understand a word they said!

Madam Alligator nudged the oldest Wet Paw. 'Take your paws out and welcome the lad.'

The oldest Wet Paw took his paws out and wiped them on his bottom. 'Welcome,' he said, still a bit slurringly. 'Here you are free to suck your paws. We shall now sing the welcome song for you!'

And they all sang,

'Wooo wooo woo wooo wooo-ooo
Wooo wooo wooo wooo
Wooo wooo woo wooo wooo-ooo
Wooo wooo wooo wooo.'

(What they meant to sing was this:
'We shall suck our paws, we shall suck our paws,
We shall suck our paws all day.
For deep in our hearts, we know the joy
Of sucking on our paws all day.')

Baghu spent a happy day on the island. The Wet Paws spent all day sucking their paws. Sometimes, they would sit down and suck their hind paws too. They never felt the need to eat, as their mouths were always busy. Baghu had never had so much fun in his life. As night fell, they found Baghu a place to sleep under the trees with them.

Soon the island was filled with the slurping sound of the Wet Paws sucking their paws. As their slurps grew louder, Baghu covered his ears with his paws and tried to sleep. But the sound was too loud and too wet.

Suddenly Baghu missed his mother. He was hungry. And the smell of fresh fish wafted in with the breeze. He got up and walked to the shore.

Madam Alligator was resting on the shore. Baghu woke her up and said, 'Please, I want to go home.'

The Wet Paws had woken up by now and came rushing to the bank. 'Ueollugh! Geullough!' said the oldest Wet Paw. (What he meant to say was: 'Don't go! Stay on!') The other Wet Paws bawled and moaned, whimpered and snivelled. But Baghu refused to listen.

Baghu jumped on to Madam Alligator's spiny back and rode back over the water that was glistening with moonlight.

SLURP!

When he reached home, he found his mother fast asleep. He snuggled up next to her and was soon fast asleep.

He woke up when the sky was just turning pink. At his side lay a huge silver fish. 'That is for you!' said his father, smiling. 'This is because you slept last night without sucking your paw at all.'

Baghu looked down at his chubby paw. And to his surprise it was absolutely dry!

Baby Green Spectacles

CHATURA RAO

Illustrated by Anitha Balachandran

One Sunday morning, Neel jumped out of bed. 'I'm going to the beach!' he shouted to his teddy bear. 'Papa is driving the Big House people for a picnic, and he's taking me along!'

Neel sat right at the back of the red jeep that took the laughing people to the beach. He didn't mind being squashed in with their bags.

When they got to the beach, Papa unloaded the picnic baskets. Neel headed straight for the water, kicking up sand as he ran.

'Don't go too far in!' Papa called.

Neel swam till he was tired. Then he sat on a rock at the water's edge. The sea swirled around it, pushing sand between his toes. The rock was green and covered with moss. It had small shells stuck on it. They were perfectly still.

Neel plucked a shell off the rock and turned it over. Out popped a brown creature. It had on a pair of round green spectacles!

'WHAT?!' it snapped.

Startled, Neel jumped to his feet. The creature plopped into the shallow water. It struggled, trying to turn on to its stomach again.

Neel heard the oddest sounds. Many, many little voices were yelling.

The shells had opened tiny doors in their shiny portions. Brown creatures wearing green spectacles popped their heads out of each. They were all talking to Neel at once!

163

One voice was louder than the rest. 'Do NOT speak all together!' it said.

The creatures fell silent, looking at the one who spoke. She was the biggest. Her brown curls were tied in a ponytail with a bit of seaweed. She wore big square spectacles on the tip of her nose. Neel thought she looked quite like his schoolteacher, Miss C. Shelly.

'Young man,' she said to Neel, 'are you going to just stand there and let Rosy struggle?'

Neel could not think of an answer.

'How can I begin the lesson,' Teacher continued, rolling her eyes, 'when one of my students is floating in the water?'

Neel bent slowly and picked Rosy up. He brought her close to his face. She was about two inches long. She looked like a tiny human baby wearing big, round glasses.

Rosy rudely stuck her tongue out at him. He quickly

put her back on the rock. Rosy scrambled to take her place. The class began.

'Now, children,' Teacher said, ignoring Neel completely. 'Answer this question: Where is the deepest water in the world?'

'Right here!' the babies chorused.

'Correct,' Teacher said. 'Which is the highest rock?'

'Mossy Rock!' they chorused again.

'And which is the best colour?'

'Brown!' they cried gleefully.

'It is not!' Neel shouted, bending close to the rock to be part of the class.

'Do NOT answer out of turn!' Teacher boomed back. 'Go sit on that rock.'

Neel climbed sulkily on. 'This is not the deepest water,' he called from his rock. 'The Pacific Ocean has the lowest seabed. Swim out and see for yourselves.'

The class gasped at this outrageous suggestion.

'And Mossy Rock is not the highest rock!' Neel stood up in excitement. 'It's just a tiny thing, like a speck of dirt on Mount Everest. That is the highest mountain in the world,' he added, raising his arms.

Teacher tried to rap him on the legs with her ruler, but he was too far away.

'And … and brown is not the best colour. Tigers are orange. They are the most awesome animals. Not little brown bugs like you!' Neel finished rudely.

The class fell silent. A little boy began to cry. Neel went close to get a look at the wailing baby.

But Teacher was not finished. 'These things you say,' she remarked, wiping her specs on her tummy, 'may be true in your classroom. But we don't believe them.'

'Why not?' Neel asked.

'Because there is no such thing as an ocean!' Teacher replied.

'And a mountain? Whatever is that?' jeered Pilu, the naughtiest boy in class.

'"Tiger" is most certainly a made-up word,' laughed Babs, a girl with spiky red hair.

Neel was furious. But before he could say a thing, Teacher thumped her ruler on the mossy rock. 'You are making it all up!' she said. 'You think you fell asleep on the sand and that this is a dream.'

Neel had to admit that he'd begun to wonder.

'However,' she said softly, leaning forward, 'we are not make-believe. So, dreamer, WAKE UP!'

Teacher whacked Neel with her ruler, right on the nose. 'Oww!' he cried, falling down.

The next moment, a huge wave crashed into him. Salt water flooded Neel's eyes. He rubbed them and struggled to sit up.

The mossy rock was bare. Neel waded around looking for the beach babies, but they had disappeared.

Then something caught his eye. A pair of square green spectacles was floating on the waves. It glinted severely at him.

Neel swam out and picked it up. He held the glass to his eye. Everything around him turned gigantic!

Mossy Rock towered over him. He floundered helplessly in the deep, deep sea. The beach, the water, the rocks, and even the sky were coloured brown.

Neel was amazed. So this was what the beach babies saw through their green spectacles!

Back home that night, Neel tucked the green specs under his pillow. 'Now Teacher will see everything in its proper size and colour,' he told his teddy bear, 'if she can see at all without her glasses!' Tired from his day's adventures, Neel fell fast asleep.

That very night, at low tide, the beach babies came back. They looked all over Mossy Rock for Teacher's spectacles. When they'd given up, Teacher took class anyway.

'It is NOT!'

'It is TOO!!'

The night rang with their arguments. The babies and their teacher just could not agree. Without her green spectacles, Teacher saw things very differently indeed!

Notes on Writers

ADITHI RAO studied theatre and film. She worked as an assistant director on the Hindi film *Satya*, and has scripted a television serial. Her first short story was published in a collection called *The Dreamer and Other Stories*.

ANITA VACHHARAJANI writes and edits children's books. She has written two books in collaboration with her artist husband.

ARTHY MUTHANNA SINGH has written eighteen books for children. She is a Senior Editor with the *Limca Book of Records* and writes for *Verve* magazine.

ASHA NEHEMIAH has written several picture books and short stories for children, including *Granny's Sari*, *The Rajah's Moustache* and *Zigzag and Other Stories*. Her books have been translated into Hindi, Assamese and Bengali.

CHATURA RAO has written for newspapers and magazines. Her first novel, *Amie and the Chawl of Colour*, was published in May 2004.

INCHOW has been writing non-fiction for adults for over a decade now. This is her first story for very young readers.

KUMKUM SOMANI is a journalist, cartoonist, playwright, teacher and scriptwriter for children's TV programmes.

MICHAEL HEYMAN has spent the last four years experiencing the heat of India while doing peripatetic research for a nonsense anthology he has edited for Penguin. He is an Associate Professor of English at Berklee College of Music in Boston, USA.

RUSKIN BOND has written over thirty books for children, including the bestselling adventures of Rusty. He lives in Mussoorie with his adopted family.

SAMIT BASU is a freelance journalist, novelist and TV scriptwriter.

SAMPURNA CHATTARJI is an award-winning poet. She has also written several books for children, including *The Greatest Stories Ever Told*.

STEPHEN AITKEN is a children's author and illustrator. His illustrated works include *The Hobyhas*, *Master Maiden* and *Odin's Journey*. To see more of Stephen's work, visit his website: www.stephenaitken.com

SWAGATA DEB is a teacher and a writer. She has translated *Goopy Gyne Bagha Byne*.

SYLVIA SIKUNDAR writes for children and young adults. She has also written resource books for teachers. She presently lives on a small island off the west coast of Canada where her water supply comes from a well and she grows her own vegetables.

VANDANA SINGH loves writing science fiction and fantasy. She also enjoys teaching college physics. Her first book for children is *Younguncle Comes to Town*.

Notes on Illustrators

AGANTUK studied at the College of Art, Delhi. He has illustrated and designed many books for children in diverse styles. He currently works with several publishing houses.

AJANTA GUHATHAKURTA studied fine arts at the College of Art, Delhi. She has illustrated many children's books and received international recognition. She is currently an illustrator and designer with Penguin Books India.

ANITHA BALACHANDRAN studied animation at the National Institute of Design, Ahmedabad. She is a photographer, illustrator and storyteller, and has worked on several children's books and films.

BINDIA THAPAR has a degree in architecture from the School of Planning and Architecture, Delhi. She has written and illustrated several books for children. Her work has been published internationally.

LOVELEEN CHAWLA is a gold medalist from the College of Art, Delhi, and is trained as an animator. She currently works with various publishing houses and agencies.

NITIN CHAWLA is an illustrator, animator and traveller at heart. He graduated from the College of Art, Delhi.

TAPOSHI GHOSHAL studied at the College of Art, Delhi. She has illustrated and designed several children's books, magazines and textbooks. She received the Kalatrayee Award from the Directorate of Education in 1985. Her work has been exhibited in India and abroad.